"You wanted me with every breath for five months."

Jewel lurched at Roque's reminder, its brutal truth, at the memory of the clawing, perpetual need that had been forced into dormancy in the past years and was now resurrected—as urgent, as tormenting. More.

His hands ran up her back, soothing her screaming tension, infusing her with far worse.

"You want me again now," he insisted.

It was pointless to deny his imperative verdict. There was every chance she'd succumb in his arms. And she wouldn't survive another such episode of sheer lunacy…

Olivia Gates has followed many dreams in her life. But there was only one she was able to pursue single-mindedly, even though it seemed the most impossible of them all: to write romance novels. The fairytale realisation of her dreams came after years of constantly learning, writing and submitting her manuscripts, when Harlequin Mills & Boon bought her first Medical Romance™. It was a dream come true, combining her passion—writing—with her vocation—medicine—in one magnificent whole. Now, living with her husband and daughter and their cat, she knows dreams are impish little things. They let you catch them only if you pursue them long and hard enough…

Recent titles by the same author:

THE HEROIC SURGEON
THE DOCTOR'S LATIN LOVER
AIRBORNE EMERGENCY

THE SURGEON'S RUNAWAY BRIDE

BY
OLIVIA GATES

™ MILLS & BOON®

Pure reading pleasure

All the characters in this book have no existence outside the imagination of the author, and have no relation whatsoever to anyone bearing the same name or names. They are not even distantly inspired by any individual known or unknown to the author, and all the incidents are pure invention.

First published in Great Britain 2007
Harlequin Mills & Boon Limited,
Eton House, 18-24 Paradise Road, Richmond, Surrey TW9 1SR

© Olivia Gates 2007

ISBN-13: 978 0 263 85265 3

Set in Times Roman 10½ on 12½ pt
03-0907-50608

Printed and bound in Spain
by Litografia Rosés, S.A., Barcelona

THE SURGEON'S RUNAWAY BRIDE

To my editor, Sheila Hodgson,
a true lady and professional.

This one is definitely for you.

Thank you for being there for me.

CHAPTER ONE

"IF IT isn't my dear, deserting wife!"

The fathomless voice hit Jewel Johansson first. The mocking tone next. The import of his statement last—and hardest.

Dear, deserting wife. *Wife?*

Her eyes shot up from the crate she was stacking. The boats gliding across Rio Solimões's muddy waters blurred, the thatch- and tin-roofed huts scattered on its banks receded, as everything was replaced by his image… *No.* Not him. Not here. *He can't be here.*

But who else would say something like that? Had a voice like that? And it was no longer just a voice, but a presence. Even after all these years, it crashed down on her. His. Him. Roque. No doubt.

And he'd called her wife, instead of *ex*-wife!

A dozen scenarios played in her mind's eye. All of them shocking her at the impulses fueling them, the volatile passions and bitterness she'd believed she no longer harbored.

Only one scenario found favor. Straightening up and walking—no, *bolting*—away. Without looking back to confirm that he was really here. She never wanted to see him again—*never*…

Stop. Breathe. Think. For whatever inconceivable—and, no doubt, transient—reason, he *was* here. So she *would* see him. Best to just face him and get it over with.

But first she needed to stress the irrelevance of his sudden reappearance. *And* locate her voluntary controls.

One thing provided the means to both ends. Pretending that loading the crate she'd been filling with medical supplies remained her priority.

Once she judged her bones had once more solidified in her limbs, she swung up, tossing her curtain of hair down her back, injecting her body language with the detachment that had been an integral part of her façade as one of the last decade's supermodels. She looked straight at him—and tears gushed in her eyes.

The blazing Brazilian midmorning sun was right at his back. Her hand came up, a belated shield against the glare and the impact of the moment of eye contact. Which didn't happen. *His* eyes were hidden behind mirrored sunglasses.

So he had her at another disadvantage. *He'd* had time to get over whatever surprise he'd felt at the sight of her, and to choose his opening shot, which had clearly been calculated for maximum disruption. And now her reaction lay bare for him to read, while his lay unfathomable behind impenetrable shields.

Sure. As if she'd ever read anything in his unshielded eyes but the passion and tenderness he'd simulated at will…

A whistle dealt her another balance-annihilating blow. "So everyone was right." A murmur followed the whistle, the elusive accent of his native Portuguese riding his seductive English delivery. "*If* not accurate. No one said you've become a goddess."

What the hell was going on here? Was that…flirtation?

She scrunched her eyes tighter, still registering only his

outline as he prowled nearer—and nearer. He gave no indication he'd stop any time soon, until she was sure he'd bump into her.

He didn't, but he stopped so near he whisper-touched her in places. His knee to her thigh, his chest to her shoulder. She staggered a step back, a dozen in her mind. Her body stood its ground, more from having no volition than from courage. He'd always been like that, brazen, sure of his effect. So he hadn't changed.

But he had. The twenty-eight-year-old sleek jaguar of a man he'd been when she'd first laid eyes on him ten years ago, who'd ruled her thoughts and decisions for the most traumatic two years of her life, had been upgraded. And how.

His leanly muscled, broad-shouldered six-foot-six frame had bulked up with maturity. The same ripening magic had taken a chisel to his face. Then he took off his sunglasses.

Everything inside Jewel jangled an all-out alarm.

"No hug for your poor abandoned husband?"

Hug. Sure. *Don't you dare shudder. And say something.*

She did. "Hi, Roque. What brings you to Tabatinga?"

She caught back a sigh of relief. That was far better than she'd expected. Steady, indifferent. Proof that his incursion hadn't provoked anything more than passing curiosity.

"'Hi, Roque.'" His mimicry was spooky, almost reproducing her voice. "Is that all I get after eight years, *minha Jóia?*"

Minha Jóia. My Jewel. He'd always called her that. Groaned it to her on the ascents of arousal, roared it from the heights of release, whispered it from the depths of satiation, branding her soul as surely as he'd branded her body and senses...

What was *wrong* with her? How could those memories be so sharp, so accessible? The territory in her being where he'd once reigned supreme was non-existent now.

"As for what I'm doing in Tabatinga…" Slanting opal eyes, which reflected the distant river and fire and sky, swept cool knowledge down her body, paused, shifted color and intensity. Her eyes followed his sweeping gaze and—God! Her drab olive shirt was plastered to breasts that, unheeding of her mental aversion, were jutting their response at his words. He had to be accessing some Pavlovian reaction she hadn't known existed! Those all-seeing eyes dwelled on the twin confessions, before going up to capture hers. "What do you think brings me all the way to the Brazilian border? Other than a burning desire to see you, *Jóia?*"

How dared he call her that now? How dared he flirt with her?

And no question, he *was* flirting. If not the offensive or hopeful propositioning other men practiced. His flirtation was laced with intimidation, his praise with menace.

That was another thing that had changed about him, then. The Roque Aguiar Da Costa she'd known had had no darkness to him, no danger. Not before their last confrontation anyway. He hadn't needed either to boost his blinding appeal. He'd reduced all females to clinging fools, not to mention vicious wildcats, without even trying. Then he'd turned it all on her and had erased her every sense of logic and self-preservation.

Well, she was no longer an emotionally starved twenty-year-old, or a damaged twenty-two-year old. She was a whole and hearty, rock-stable thirty-year-old professional and he was interrupting a job she'd been preparing for a year. She wanted him to vanish on that account alone.

"So you traveled 2500 miles from Rio de Janeiro to the Brazilian-Colombian border to see me? Well, now you have seen me." She upped her coldness factor, gave him the practiced dismissal she'd perfected in her former trade. "Anything else I can do for you?"

"Plenty."

His flagrant innuendo hit hard. *Don't let him bait you. Don't even try to guess why he wants to. End this.*

She hiked all the height she could in her five-foot-eleven frame, disconcerted yet again at the rare event of being towered over. "OK, Roque, this was fun, but whatever you're here for…"

A cacophony of approaching shouts sent the snub she hadn't yet formulated in her mind backlashing in her throat.

She swung around to the source of disturbance, registered only the outline of a truck screeching to a halt against the glare. Until the dust it had kicked up settled, she choked on the relief of interruption, of reprieve. On the gall that she should feel it, that he could affect her that much—still.

Which didn't matter right now. Right now she was needed. She recognized cries for help when she heard them.

Indigenous people poured from the decrepit vehicle and rushed toward her and Roque, yelling an indecipherable jumble of a local dialect and Portuguese. She understood one word. Snakebite.

She didn't need more explanations. She had to get to her emergency supplies, to the casualty. And Roque was in her way!

He was running ahead of her, his longer legs sustaining his lead no matter how much speed she poured on. He jumped on board her boat first, bent and scooped her by the waist up the two-foot haul. He released her before she could process his scalding touch, his actions. Dazed, she rushed inside after him and confusion turned to chagrin when his bulk kept blocking her path all the way to the treatment room.

"Move out of my way, Roque." She pushed at him, anxious to get to her patient.

He only turned, revealing that no casualty had been brought

in. His lips twisted at her bewilderment. "You didn't get the part where they said we had to go to the casualty?"

"*We?* They came here seeking *my* help."

Daunting eyebrows rose, a portrait of sarcasm. "Yours? And you know that when you didn't even understand what they said?"

"I know because the residents have been running to us with every medical complaint they have since they found out we were a medical expedition, and to me specifically as I'm the leader. We'll handle it, so don't feel like you have to help here. I'm sure you have more important things to do."

"You're suggesting there's anything more important than a person in danger? And that I can disregard such a person to keep up with my schedule? What kind of doctor do you think I am?"

The last part dripped with that baiting tone. She bit back a retort. *The worst kind. The mercenary, exploitative kind.*

Better leash it in, give him no more reasons to stick around and extend this—this…*whatever* this was, out of spite.

She gave him her most diplomatic look. "The best kind, I'm sure. You're just not needed here. So why don't you get out now and let me do my job?" So much for diplomacy.

"Move out of my way, Roque. Get out, Roque," he mimicked again. Another chameleon power, that uncanny ability to change his voice. If not as uncanny as the way his eyes changed color. Or the way he'd changed his disposition to whatever suited his purpose. "Is that any way to talk to a godsend in this emergency? What's next? Go jump in the river, Roque?"

Her resistance crumbled. She gave up any pretense of civility, and swallowed his bait. "As long as you don't resurface so you can continue wasting my time. Just how are you a godsend? Last time I looked you were a surgeon, not an emergency doctor."

He met her exasperation with mockery. "And last time I looked you were in front of the cameras selling haute couture."

"Your memory must be going. The last time you looked, the only cameras I was in front of were X-ray and MRI ones."

Silence crashed. Damn. She shouldn't have made reference to the past. That gave it relevance. Rawness. Gave him ammunition.

But, wonder of wonders, he didn't use it. Instead, he turned to the supplies cabinets lining the wall. He snatched up a lock, swung back to her. "Keys?" he demanded.

She fumed, rustled for them in her cargo pants pockets, chaos pushing to the surface. How did he know his way around here? How long had he been here, snooping around behind her back?

He was clearly providing no answers. Or space. He didn't budge, forcing her to squeeze against him to open the cabinets. She didn't jerk away. She wouldn't give him the display of discomfort he was after. Discomfort? Try upheaval.

Angrier at herself than at him, she snatched extra supplies, stuffed them with unnecessary force into the main emergency bag as her totally unwanted and unexpected partner checked the airway bag and added articles to it, too. She was dragging the zipper closed when his hand clamped hers. She jerked this time.

He met her fury with cool calculation. "Snakes common here are the hemotoxic *jararaca* and the neurotoxic *surucucu pico de jaca*. Do you have specific antivenins for those species?"

She did a double-take. A city surgeon like him shouldn't be versed in Brazilian jungle reptilian dwellers or be aware that snake venom actually came in two varieties—the hemotoxic variety that caused death from uncontrolled bleeding and the neurotoxic one that caused death by paralysis of breathing muscles.

So. Score one for his wilderness medicine knowledge. It couldn't be as extensive as hers. Not with the intensive course she'd had at the Jungle Warfare Training Center in Manaus.

Roque's grip still demanded an answer. *Just give it to him.* She yanked her hand away and the zipper closed. "I have coral snake antivenins and crotalidae polyvalent antivenin."

He again stopped her from hiking the bag over her shoulder, his eyes pinning her, probing. "No Cro-Fab?"

So his knowledge extended to the new, purified antivenin of sheep origin. How nice. "Alas, not at seven hundred dollars per vial. Global Aid Organization—our expedition sponsors—are scraping by nowadays."

He gave a slow nod, pressed on. "If we need the polyvalent antivenin, are you stocked up on anti-anaphylaxis drugs?"

That *had* to be freshly acquired knowledge for whatever purpose had brought him here. Why would his brain be cluttered with such unnecessary data for a surgeon? He couldn't have always known polyvalent antivenin could elicit hypersensitivity reactions, from chronically debilitating to instantly fatal.

And *of course* she was prepared! "I have a comprehensive kit." She snarled her displeasure.

It didn't even loosen his grip. "You have a surgical kit, too? Surgical intervention is a possibility here."

"Which part of *comprehensive* didn't you understand?"

He just shrugged. "I understand comprehensive one way and an internist—like the one you are nowadays—would another, *Jóia.*"

So he knew exactly what she was now. Of course he did. It felt like long-established knowledge, too. No time to wonder how, when and why. She snatched the bag open, stabbed a finger at the set of surgical instruments and materials.

Satisfied at last, he reached out urgent hands to take the

bag's considerable weight from her. She wrestled him for it and it was his turn to glower. But he said nothing, just turned and sprinted out of the boat. The moment he jumped off, his arms reached up to help her down. She avoided them, hugged the bag high as she negotiated the uneven stairs. He reached up and hauled her down to the pier, bag and all.

His touch was imperative, practical and gone in seconds—along with the bag. Her heart still fired randomly and wildfire radiated from every point of contact with his fingers to engulf her body. This was getting ridiculous! *Snakebite casualty. Get to it.*

With the burden of the bag removed from her, she ran to the truck. Inácio and Madeline, her friends and assistants, were already on board. Roque beat her there, jumped into the open truck bed, as silent and agile as a big cat, and again bent to her, hauled her with great ease, and care, all the way up.

Before she found a footing, the wheels shrieked, kicked up a storm of the red soil Tabatinga was named after, then the vehicle lurched forward. She was catapulted backwards, found nothing at her back, saw Roque receding, the world blurring by. Panic burst, hot, desperate—then it was over, dissipating within the same booming heartbeat. Roque had snatched her back!

Her fingers dug a blind anchor into him, stifling a cry as the sudden deceleration drove a lance through her neck.

Impossibly steady, he herded her to the only empty corner in the truck's long bed where he pulled her down and came down beside her, enclosing her between his bulk and the truck's side, making sure its violent heaves had minimum effect on her.

Her dazed eyes searched his face, read nothing but his intent to ensure her comfort. A jumble of reactions churned inside her as he relinquished her eyes, turned to the tribesmen.

What did he think she was? A swooning damsel who needed to be handed in and out of carriages? Did he think she retained any part of the susceptible girl she'd been before her accident, or the disturbed and even more pliable one after it?

Embarrassed acknowledgement followed indignation. He had saved her from a nasty tumble, and no doubt a new set of injuries.

But a surge of illicit pleasure dominated everything. At all his courtesies, at their grace and effortlessness.

God. Just how stupid could she get? Courtesies? She was fluttering at those? Courtesies had no place between them. They'd parted on the worst of terms. They no longer owed each other consideration. So why was he offering any now?

And why was she wondering? He'd always been thoughtful before, overwhelmingly so at times. It had felt so sincere then, too. And it had all been a means to an end.

So what did his gestures mean now? What did his presence here mean? Did he want something from her still? What *could* he want this time? Was this about his American citizenship? Was her absence holding up finalizing procedures—or something…?

"Now I understand why they didn't bring the victim to us." His spine-tingling baritone yanked her out of her oppressive musings. "This isn't a recent bite. The victim is their shaman and yesterday they found him in the jungle ill and delirious. They didn't interfere, fearing he might be under some self-induced trance as part of his rituals, which confused the picture. Today he deteriorated and they finally examined him and found the fang marks."

Her eyebrows shot up, impressed he could understand the tribesmen's obscure language in such detail. "So our debate over antivenins was for nothing. We've long missed the four-hour window when they could have inactivated the venom. What took them so long to seek help? And why seek help at all? Indigenous people are very good at handling snakebites."

Roque's frown showed his aggravation. "Like so many other tribes here, this one is no longer what you can call indigenous. They are now of mixed ethnicity and have for generations been exposed to different cultures through their association with the drug-involved narco-guerillas and their intermarriages with Portuguese-origin Brazilians, which, it seems, have not been to their advantage. But apparently the one thing they cling to from their indigenous roots is the superstitions. Their shaman's mystical-spiritual status is warping their decision-making. Even after they decided to seek help, they didn't dare move him. And by the way—they say if he dies we'll be punished."

She sighed. "That's standard practice with some tribes."

He inclined his head, leaning back for a better overall look at her. "And the threats don't worry you?"

"Oh, they don't. I discovered they're all talk."

"Then you'd be alone in believing that. The clinic staff at the platoon outpost take such threats seriously. They're no longer willing to offer the people around here such reputedly punishable-by-death help. That's why they ran to *us*."

She ignored the emphasized "us", and cast a skeptical look at the men who didn't look all that threatening right now. "Maybe the clinic staff are just swamped."

He shook his head. "They're not swamped, they're wary. This region is almost ungovernable. The Brazilian army's Frontier Command, which they belong to, is responsible for security along a whopping 850 miles of open frontier with Colombia and Peru. Serving over a hundred thousand people, with the foreigners among them mostly into drug trafficking and illegal fishing and logging, it wouldn't be smart to risk themselves on humanitarian gestures. Smart would be believing a threat when they hear one."

She knew all that, but was stunned that he did. She'd always wondered how most people were uninformed about their own country, how foreigners who'd made it their home, like she'd made Brazil, knew far more about it than they did. But it seemed he wasn't only informed about his country, but insightful, comprehensive, passionate. This didn't sit well with the kind of person she'd always thought he was.

She shrugged, escaped her own deductions. "I only speak from experience when I say such threats amount to nothing."

He pouted his skepticism. "Maybe you managed to avoid their wrath because you have succeeded in curing them so far."

She leaned back, putting more breathable air between them. "There were times I didn't. No. Issuing the threats always felt like some sort of tradition or something, insurance to stop strangers messing where they don't belong, or promising what they can't deliver. But from my experience they're actually very kind and welcoming people and when you help them, they're just thankful, and very demonstrative about it. Proof is that I haven't been killed or maimed yet for failing to save any…"

The rest jammed in her throat. At the word 'maimed', his eyes ignited, poured what felt like lava over her skin as they traced her now-vanished scars. His hand followed suit and something she'd long thought rock-stable inside her wrenched loose.

She struggled not to lurch away as his fingers lingered where once a half-inch scar had run vertically down from her left eyebrow to the corner of her jaw, a scar he'd fondled and tormented on endless nights of abandon. She'd hated him for that most of all. For pretending not to be repulsed by her, manipulating her hypersensitive physical and emotional scars.

Now those fingers that had once been all over her weaved in her hair, caressing a heavy lock behind her ear. Had it caught fire? Had her skin?

She did lurch when he spoke, moaned at the stab of pain in her neck. "You talk as if you've been here a long time…" She shouldn't have heard his whisper above the truck's din. It was all she heard. "When I know you've been here only a few days."

What more did he know about her? Everything? She pressed back into the truck, tried to suppress the tremors racking her body, tried to knead away the twinge in her neck. "I've been in many places in the rainforest. I expect the same laws apply."

He kept on talking, matter-of-fact, as if he wasn't taking over kneading her neck, pouring ease into fresh pain and nine-year-old aches. "They don't. The border with Colombia is the most paranoid place in the country. Those who live here have become hardened by the constant dangers and their reactions are tinged by the extremism that stems from fear and ignorance."

His fingertips located the exact point of pain, spread relief, and longings she'd thought she'd forgotten.

She wouldn't moan. She wouldn't! She gasped instead, "Are you saying these people mean their threat?"

He flashed her a harsh smile. "They can mean it all they like. I'm not about to leave a man to die because of idiotic threats. And I'm not about to let them near you either."

A harsh thrill shot down her spine. This chivalry *had* to be an act. "Oh, so you're not included in the threat?"

"I can take care of myself, *minha Jóia*."

Her lips compressed. "And you think I can't?"

"Not like I can." Before steam vented from her ears, he caught her hand. "And then I have something you don't…"

He dragged it inside his multi-pocketed vest, over his rock-like abdomen, then lower. Before she could snatch her already burning hand away, she felt it. A gun. A monster by the feel of it.

Her eyes rounded. "Are you into black ops now?"

"I just find it moronic to parade unprepared into areas where known danger lurks."

"We do have armed guards on our expedition. And they're right behind us in that Jeep."

He cast said Jeep an amused look. "And I should do what, in your opinion? Squeal for their help if the need arises?"

A laugh burst out of her at the incongruous image of all this virility squealing for any reason. He laughed with her. Then just as suddenly he sobered. Time and space warped then vanished. She no longer registered the men who sat huddled and apprehensive at the other end of the truck or her assistants, who were watching her and Roque in utter fascination.

His eyes overflowed with something that accessed all the uncontainable passion that had once swallowed her whole. Tension blasted off him, congealing the air around them, sending awareness like she'd never felt, even with him, shrieking down her nerves, tangible and tormented.

"We're here, people." Madeline's voice shattered her trance. Then everything else crashed back into her awareness.

They'd come to a stop in a huge clearing surrounded by huts. Dozens of men and women dressed in a haphazard mix of modern clothes and tribal beads and paint were already ringing their truck, faces and hands anxious, hurrying them along.

And she was panting, trembling. Roque was breathing hard, too, his eyes as disturbed as hers must be.

An endless moment later he finally rasped, "Later, Jewel."

Then he freed her from his thrall, snapped up to his feet,

bent to assist her. This time she gave him the hand he demanded eagerly, let it drown in the safety and support of his all the way to their emergency.

Why not, when there'd be no later? When this was an outtake from time that would end as soon as the unnatural extension of the emergency did?

Then he'd be gone and she'd rebury his memory, along with the miscarried baby she'd borne him.

CHAPTER TWO

ROQUE had to hand it to Jewel. She could bury anything.

She'd once buried her true nature so deep he hadn't even suspected it. She'd buried her opinion of him so well it had been a devastating shock and a lasting scar when it had resurfaced. And now she'd buried her agitation so completely he wondered if he'd imagined it. But no—he *had* gotten to her.

If not as badly as she'd gotten to him. He hadn't expected this, had he? He hadn't even intended to do this, to approach her this way, to taunt her—to touch her. But he'd laid eyes on her and hadn't been in control of his actions ever since… *Get to business,* idiota! *And take control this time.*

As the far more experienced doctor, he was the triage officer here, and should decide how to handle their patient, delegate responsibilities. It wasn't the first time he'd been forced to rely on unknowns in the field, and he'd had everything from disastrous to outstanding incidental assistants. He had no reason to believe Jewel would be on the favorable side of that spectrum. She seemed to have good theoretical knowledge and came well prepared with GAO's comprehensive kits, but that augured nothing for her clinical powers.

Not that she lacked confidence. In the seconds they'd been

in Qircamo the shaman's hut, she'd already started resuscitation, not even thinking of deferring to his superior experience. From her attitude so far, it seemed she didn't believe *that* existed, or was relevant here. She seemed to believe surgeons lacked the necessary skills to handle emergencies. While *she* did, of course.

It also seemed her assistants shared her confidence in her abilities. Or maybe they were obeying their medical hierarchy programming, with nurse always deferring to doctor. Inácio Lima, a fellow Brazilian he knew to be a trauma nurse packing an extensive ten-year field track record, had already crouched into her assistant's position unquestioningly.

It left him with a choice to pull rank, take this part of management over, or let her do the preliminaries and tend to the bite site himself. Which was no choice really. Any medic could handle the ABCs. His expertise was better reserved for handling the trauma. And he'd better get to that before Madeline O'Brien, Jewel's other nurse, took it on herself to do it.

He took his place by Qircamo's legs, murmured to Madeline delineating his needs. As she jumped to it, at once recognizing a more specialized medical person, he heard Jewel murmuring hers to Inácio. In flawless Portuguese.

His eyes snapped up in shock. Had that effortless flow really issued from her? During the five months of their marriage, she'd barely learned two dozen words!

So, it seemed once she'd left him, learning Portuguese hadn't remained the painful obligation it had been when he'd tried to teach it to her. And he couldn't *believe* the gush of disappointment this knowledge provoked.

He suppressed the stupid reaction, dragged his focus back to his patient as Madeline exposed the patient's leg. Then nothing could have torn it away from the sight of one of a surgeon's worst nightmares—a bloated, discolored limb. And nothing could ameliorate his dismay at seeing the reason for it. A tourniquet!

And not just any tourniquet, a tight one, midway down the thigh, hoping to stop the flow of a poison that had long been circulating in the man's system by the time they'd applied it. All it had achieved had been the current dismal-looking prognosis. This was compartment syndrome that was teetering on the edge of gangrene.

"Scissors." His growl made Madeline jump, brought every eye in the hut, starting with Qircamo's people, who'd insisted on attending their treatment, slamming into him. He sheared off the catastrophic piece of meticulously applied fabric and almost roared at the sight of the messy, suppurating wound. Dammit. All signs said he could be too late…

Damn the signs. And damn these people. If they didn't know how to manage snakebite they should have at least have known how not to compound its dangers! Had their tribal medicine knowledge vanished totally?

His blood tumbled in futility. He knew the answer to this one. They'd been corrupted, cut off from their origins with no new knowledge to replace that they were losing, or had already lost. Most of the shamans and medicine men, the living repositories of their knowledge, were over seventy years old, with no one left in their tribes interested in taking on their mantles. As they died out so did everything vital to those people's survival. And here lay Qircamo, one of those precious people, dying, thanks to his flock's ignorance and confusion.

Madeline noted the extensive bruising around the wound and the bleeding from his mouth and nose, indicating severe hemotoxic envenomation. He didn't need to hear Inácio announcing the blood-pressure reading to know the shaman had severe hypotension, didn't need bleeding-clotting tests to know coagulation was shot to hell.

"Any chance the antivenin might reverse the symptoms and compartment syndrome now?" he heard Inácio murmuring to Jewel.

Good question, as it usually did. Just not this late in the day. Before he could say so, Jewel delivered her verdict.

"Not this long after the bite." So she knew it, too.

Roque shot off a list of all the instruments he'd need to resolve the compartment syndrome by deeply incising between the leg's muscular compartments to relieve the building pressure inside them that was cutting off circulation. He sat back on his heels as Madeline spread his requested items on a double layer of prepacked surgical towels, his focus back on Jewel.

She'd already handed back the battery-operated suction machine to Inácio. She must have already cleared the airway of secretions. He now watched her deft movements as she assembled the laryngoscope, asking for a specific size endotracheal tube.

Not going for rapid-sequence anesthesia before intubation, eh? Sound decision, Roque decided. The man's consciousness was depressed enough, he wouldn't resist or gag on the ET. And it would be foolish to test his precarious general condition by adding potent drugs to the mix. That was also why he was going for a local anesthetic nerve block for his procedure.

He rummaged through the syringes for various needle lengths. Hmm. No six-inch needles. He'd have to do with a four-inch one, then. He hoped it would be enough to reach the sciatic nerve through the swollen limb. He filled the syringe with lidocaine and snapped a look up. And did a stunned double-take.

It had been less than thirty seconds and Jewel had already intubated Qircamo. *And* had a gastric tube in, too. *Very* good.

Then she began delivering positive pressure ventilation with one hundred percent oxygen, and how she did *that* took his assessment of her emergency medicine skills from very good to superior. Not enough field doctors knew the necessity of initial hyperventilation to maximize oxygen saturation, or of giving ventilations slowly, over two to three seconds each. She did it all with textbook precision.

Having taken care of airway and breathing, she turned to Inácio who was handling circulation. "That's A and B. How's C?"

Inácio shook his head. "His veins are totally collapsed."

Jewel pursed her lips. "OK. Let's get central."

Unease raced down Roque's spine. It was true that if peripheral access through superficial arm veins, the method of choice to rehydrate shocked patients, failed, nothing was faster than central venous access. Yet an easier and far safer way was a venous cut-down. Cutting the skin over a superficial vein in the ankle needed far less expertise and had none of CVA's risks of injuring the major arteries and nerves that ran intimately with deep veins. *He* could do a CVA blindfolded. And he would.

It surprised him that he didn't relish the idea of stepping in and taking over. And before he did so, he wanted to know why she opted for the hard route. Handling intubation—and not a particularly tricky one—was all well and good. CVA was tricky at the best of times. This was one of the worst times on record.

"Why didn't you opt for a cut-down?" he asked.

Jewel's eyes rose briefly at his question before they lowered to her chore once more. "I'd rather not traumatize his healthy leg. And having a central line in would enable us to monitor his circulation in response to our intervention far better than other pressure measurements. *As* I'm sure you know."

Her challenge sent a spurt of stimulation fizzing in his blood, which made him counter, "We'll inject him with a megadose of antibiotics and tetanus toxoid so the possibility of infection in his uninjured leg will be beyond minimal..."

"But there, nonetheless."

He plowed on. "And cut-down is far less problematic."

"Not in his specific condition. He may lose one leg. I'd rather keep the other one untouched."

She'd defended her decision well. Was she really up to it?

He challenged her again. "You have to consider the high possibility of injury to arteries and nerves. An arterial injury now can be fatal. In inexperienced hands..."

Her eyes flashed gold. "There are none of those here. Why don't you see to the part you took over? Better still, why don't you try again to take our audience outside and I'll finish access in a minute and do the procedure myself?"

He really shouldn't be enjoying this, and so much. Not now. Later, he planned on reveling in the unexpectedness of it all. Yet the very devil rode him to say, "That's a surgeon's job."

He could almost see her sticking out her mental tongue. "I'm sure that's what you've been always told in the exalted seclusion of your surgical realm."

With that she dismissed him and turned back to her procedure. His eyes clung to her every move as Madeline prepped the surgery field and draped Qircamo, ready to intervene at the first sign of trouble. What he got was trouble breathing.

With a confidence that could have been born of nothing but

extreme familiarity with the procedure, she blindly located the subclavian vein with the needle. Not even going for the internal jugular, eh? She went for the better but far harder choice, and in less than a minute had the catheter in and secured in place.

Roque let out the breath he'd been holding, inhaled another to order the administration of a mannitol bolus to expand Qircamo's blood volume rapidly. The words slid down his throat unuttered. She was doing just that. This was getting weird.

As mind-boggling as it still was, he'd long known Jewel had become a doctor and had been roaming his country with GAO for three years now. But doctors came in all levels of skill and he'd had no reason to believe she'd be a skilled one. He'd even worked it out that her being with GAO was against her, not the other way around. In today's world they were so desperate for every volunteer that their once highest standards could be slipping. But that had been unequivocal skill he'd just witnessed. And then some.

And it left him more confused than ever. He'd already been at a loss to explain how the top model he'd known, or the traumatized girl he'd married, had become a doctor at all. The best explanation, and a shaky one, was that she'd been around doctors so long after her accident, had learned so much, that she'd just decided to become one and be done with it…

"All ready, Dr. er…"

His gaze dragged back to Madeline. They hadn't had time for the barest of introductions. She and Inácio had taken their cue from their boss, assuming she knew what she was doing, inviting him along, must have gathered she knew *him* intimately…

"Dr. Aguiar Da Costa at your service. But that's just for reference. Call me Roque." He felt the electrifying caress of Jewel's gaze sweeping him. He raised eager eyes for a direct feel, and there it was again—that blast of affinity. And he'd spent eight years reassuring himself he'd always imagined it!

He couldn't resist asking. "I'm going to perform a double-incision fasciotomy. Would you like to assist me, *Jóia?*"

She gave a tiny start at his offer. Then her eyes narrowed. She suspected his motives. What did she think? That he wanted to prove she'd overstated her abilities? She wouldn't be far from the truth. The average internist would at best have knowledge of fasciotomy but no experience with performing it. And though average and Jewel couldn't be put in the same sentence together, this *was* beyond her expected skills, no matter how good she was.

Her eyes searched his for the trap for two more seconds then she nodded to Madeline. The latter made way for her at once, handing her a mask and gloves. They were a good team. Fluent, at ease, yet keeping the correct amount of respect and distance for each other's respective expertise and position.

Jewel donned her surgical garb and settled into position facing him. "What kind of nerve block are you going for?"

"What kind would you go for?"

One dense, dark eyebrow arched up. "What's this? A test?"

"If I'm going to be counting on your assistance, can you blame me for wanting to assess your capabilities?"

She gritted her teeth. "There's no time for your nonsense."

"We haven't and we aren't wasting time," he countered. "It's been exactly eight minutes since we stepped in here."

She exhaled as she snatched the syringe out of his hand. "Why don't I give you a demonstration?" She crowded him until he made way for her. "Maybe I can teach you a thing or two about a combined sciatic-lumbar plexus three-in-one nerve block."

Stimulation kicked higher in his blood. "Teach me, then."

And she did. Taught him she was even better than she'd boasted.

After she'd injected the anesthetic, they used the time until it worked to reassess resuscitation and prepare the plaster splint they'd need at the end of the procedure. Then it started.

He made a six-inch incision over the anterior leg to provide adequate visualization. Then he dissected the subcutaneous tissues for wide exposure of the leg compartments while Jewel blotted out blood and oozing fluid, anticipated and interacted with his needs and moves with a fluency that brought his eyes back to her mask and cap-covered face over and over again.

After he'd finished the first stage, she murmured, "Going for a transverse incision to expose the lateral intermuscular septum and superficial peroneal nerve?"

Another spurt of surprised approval tugged at his lips beneath his mask. On impulse, he made room for her to perform that step. Without missing a beat, she took over and did it. No doubt about it. She'd done this many times before. He wondered when she'd had the time to amass such experience.

As soon as she was done, he took over again. As he made more incisions, releasing pressure, restoring circulation, Jewel retracted veins and nerves, cleared his field and helped him prepare for his next move as if they'd always worked together, until he almost forgot they hadn't always done so.

He ended the surgical part of the procedure, asked, "What next?" Post-procedural measures were critical to prognosis and it was usually where physicians slackened. This was where he might uncover a chink in her knowledge. And he couldn't believe how reluctant he was to uncover any. He should relish it!

To his chagrined relief, none was uncovered. She answered by practically making all the right decisions, packing the wound, leaving it open to drain, then applying Vessiloops, rubber bands that approximated the wound sides to prevent skin retraction. Inácio handed him the splint and he fitted it along the calf with the ankle held at 90 degrees.

Another assessment revealed what he'd only hoped for. Qircamo was stabilizing, with definite pulses in his leg.

Breathing again in immense relief, Roque announced the happy news to the tribe. And just as they'd been threatening and suspicious before, they were as over-zealously grateful now, sweeping their newfound heroes into an inescapable tribute.

Two hours later, stuffed with exotic offerings, Roque's impromptu team made their escape to the truck. He walked beside Jewel, watched her as he had all through the feast, her every nuance sending his senses rioting, accessing every overriding memory he'd thought long erased. He was close enough to count her shallow breaths, the beads of sweat clinging like gems to her upper lip. His hands and tongue tingled. His heart itched. Especially now he felt how drained she was.

Once he'd settled her in the truck she turned her eyes up to his. "Think we'll need to return in a couple of days for wound closure, or debridement of more devitalized tissue—or worse?"

Worse would be amputation. And though he usually had an accurate prognosis by now, he had no answer to anything. Not after fighting for that man's life with the last woman he'd ever thought to do it with. It meant anything was possible.

A surge of optimism fueled his answer. "*Jóia,* I think our shaman still has a lot of walking in the jungle to do."

Her gaze wavered before she dropped it. "I guess so." Then she exhaled. "It was really good to have you with us in this."

Instead of being warmed by her admission, it was like

being doused in ice. In acid. It brought back all the disparagement she'd slashed him with before she'd walked out on him.

At length, he drawled, "I have my uses, don't I? Though that's not one of the uses you thought I was good for, is it? Eight years ago you *told* me what you thought me good for—sex and marriage. The first for your own titillation, and having one up on the amoral, disturbed women in your circle. The other as your best revenge on your snooty parents and cheating ex-fiancé—marrying the one man it had horrified them most to see you with."

He watched her face drain of life.

When she finally spoke, her voice was equally lifeless. "It was too much to expect us to remain civil now the crisis is over. At least we won't suffer each other's presence much longer."

"And you're sure about that?"

Her gaze flared, wavered. Then it steadied again. "We can stay out of each other's way for the couple of days it will take to complete Qircamo's treatment." She cocked her head at him. "But you didn't say what you're really doing here…" She paused at his sardonic pout, gave a dismissive wave. "Forget it. It's none of my business."

"Just idle curiosity, eh? But even that can be really painful if unappeased. Surely you must have theories."

She shrugged. "None. Besides the indigenous tribes, frontier settlers and Brazilian army Frontier Command platoons who make up the population, passers-by are tourists, illegal loggers or miners, smugglers, guerillas, fugitives and—for the first time—people like my team. Surgeons don't frequent this place."

So cool. But he'd already glimpsed the inferno he'd once burned in, had been deprived of. He wanted more. Now.

His knee nudged her thigh. She pulled away. His hand

anchored gently into her flesh, burning at the contact. "A very systematic deduction-elimination technique. So you can't believe me burning up with the desire to see you as a motive, *Jóia?* What would you believe, then? That I'm here to work? That would be true, too. I'm here to join the expedition."

An incredulous laugh ripped from her. "Go ahead. Pull the other one. No way in hell are you joining my expedition!"

He gave her a mock contrite look. "You've got me there. You're right, I'm not joining the expedition. I'm *leading* it."

CHAPTER THREE

"SURPRISE."

His eyes glided over her flushing, stiffening features, saw denial following shock there. Then contempt rounded up the explicit display. She'd written off his declaration as an obnoxious attempt to pull her leg.

Then she stated her conclusion. "Nice try, Roque. It would be a balmy day in hell the day you're my leader.".

Exhilaration coursed through his system. "Is it the word 'leader' you object to? Want to call me something else? 'Chief' maybe? Personally, I prefer 'boss'. Crooned by that voice of yours…" He left the explicit imagery up to her memory, his gaze sweeping over her, no longer deliberate, succumbing to the pleasure of absorbing her exquisiteness. And her ratcheting agitation.

"I'm not calling you anything at all!"

He moved closer, re-establishing contact with her. "Then don't call me anything, *meu bela*. Touch me instead."

Her pupils almost filled her cat's-eye-like irises. "Drop the cheap seduction act, Roque." Her voice was husky, tight.

Not as tight as he was. Head, chest and loins. Her voice—it had echoed in his head, attacking him with sudden clarity over the years, creating the illusion of her proximity at times when it had done the most damage. He'd added to her sins with each onslaught. But it had lost its languid, reticent overtones, became more hard-hitting. Or maybe he'd never heard her in hot-blooded anger before. He could get used to this.

He went after more, provoked her, with both tone and touch. "Who says it's an act, *belleza?*"

She gasped, and he almost did. Unbelievable. The people around them went unnoticed. The dozen reasons for antipathy lying between them went unheeded. So her effect on him hadn't been an exaggerated memory. But at least back then he'd been a moonstruck fool who'd believed he loved her. Now he despised her. Shouldn't that dampen his reaction? Apparently not.

He got out his cellphone, tugged her stiff, sweaty hand, exerted enough power to keep her from pulling it away, to place the phone there. "Call GAO Central and confirm my appointment."

She stared at the phone for a couple more moments before she drew in a tremulous inhalation and hit the dial button. She kept those unique eyes that he'd convinced himself he'd banished from his every fantasy focused on the screen.

Those eyes—they'd once made him ready to lose a limb to make her whole again. They were now filled with frustration and fury. And shock as she got confirmation of what he'd said.

He tried to savor the emotions kicking inside him. Relish? Triumph? So why didn't they feel good? Feel good? He'd no longer know what "feel good" felt like if it rammed him in the gut….

Anger rose again. He was entitled to satisfaction, snatching this from her. So why couldn't he damn well enjoy it?

He knew why. It was what he saw in those eyes. Panic.

Sim, certamente. As if the woman who'd traveled the most dangerous regions of his vast country, the one who'd gone under the scalpel electively so many times, who'd just braved the threats of superstitious, desperate people, would fear anything.

But she *was* distressed. He should relish *that*.

But he didn't. He hated seeing her distressed, hated more being the source of her distress. *Deus,* he was pathetic. And this after the thousand scenes he'd imagined since she'd walked out on him, of how he'd feel on the event of their "reunion."

But she hadn't only walked out on him. She'd left him struggling with the loss of their unborn baby, with knowing why she hadn't wanted it. And ever since then, he'd projected. Then he'd laid eyes on her again and all his conjectures had evaporated.

He would have been content if it had been pure lust he'd felt. It, too, was ugly and cold and indifferent. But what he'd felt had stunned him. He'd just felt…*happy* to see her.

It had to be her beauty. Surgery had restored it then time had ripened it. That *must* explain the same sledgehammer effect.

But it *wasn't* the same. She wasn't. In the past, she'd trembled at his approach, melted at his touch. Now she'd dismissed him, challenged him, the haughtiness he'd only tasted when she'd had enough of him elevated to an art.

But there was something else besides the new fire and cool hauteur. Before there'd been silk running through her, a malleability that had driven him to extremes to protect her. Now there was steel. He'd seen how deep it ran through her during Qircamo's procedure. Had it been bestowed by her ordeals? Or had it always been there and he'd just been oblivious to it?

But he was sure one thing was totally new. The assurance of experience.

An experience that extended to men?

Deus! What was that acrid taste? Jealousy? How stupid would that be? They'd both lived their lives since their explosive, short-lived marriage had ended.

So you call the attempts to rid yourself of her taste in other women's arms living your life? an inner voice mocked.

No. That had been a waste. His work had been, and remained, the only living he did. And there he surely lived to the full.

She ended the taut phone call, turned stiffly to him.

"So it's true." She handed back his phone. He closed his hand over hers as he took it. She gritted her teeth. "All I want to know now is how you managed it. And why. This is my project!"

He shrugged lazily. "I know, and I must congratulate you on a job well done in setting it up." And this was nothing but the truth. She'd gone above and beyond the call of duty. "Your stage is truly set."

Her exquisite eyebrows drew together. "Stage? What stage? Is this some sort of metaphor?"

"We both know what stage, *Jóia.* It's self-evident."

"Not to me," she said through gritted teeth. "*Do* explain the obvious!"

Anyone would believe she had no idea what he was talking about. Very convincing. As convincing as the melancholy and vulnerability that had so clashed with her voluptuousness, that had turned his attraction into obsession. He now realized it had been a trick for the cameras, her claim to fame. That it had become real after her accident was beside the point.

But in the past hours there'd been no hint of that sadness that had driven him to excesses to erase. She'd surely changed.

If not for the better! Her obsession with regaining her beauty betrayed her need to make the leap back into the spotlight. And she'd found an ingenious way that was a hundred times more effective than modeling. A reality show starring the world's first doctor who was also an adventurer, an explorer, a humanitarian worker and a woman as alluring as a movie star.

And that was why he was here. To stop her exploiting this expedition and his people for her own ends.

"Well?"

Her sharp, imperative tone made him grit his teeth. "You have a film crew along, don't you?"

"Huh…?" She gaped at his counter-question. Then she shook her head. "There's any logic to this out-of-the-blue question?"

His lips twisted in a sneer. "I have to give it to you—the concept is ground-breaking. As many expeditions as there are into the Brazilian rainforest, none have been undertaken to reach the isolated tribes of the Vale do Javari region to diagnose and treat the diseases that pose a threat to their survival. And I just happen to know your purpose behind this worthy endeavor."

He knew all there was to know about her since she'd left him. Though her personal life remained obscure, as if she had none… He exhaled, stifled foolish conjectures.

"And what the hell *is* this 'purpose' that you make sound so sinister?" she seethed.

"Add yourself, a film crew, the Amazon and endangered people to the concerns GAO have about the nature and purpose of the 'documentary' you've included as an integral part of this expedition, and the result is clear. An unprecedented pilot to launch a blockbusting reality show."

It was her turn to stare. And stare. Heat blasted off her, scorching him with her soaring anger. Was she mad that he'd found her out? An explosive denial was sure to follow.

Sure enough, she finally erupted, "A reality show? This is what you think I'm doing here?"

He gave her his best baiting smile. "It's not?"

"Damn straight it's not. Of all the moronic ideas! And this is why you're here? To join the show? Taking over my project...?"

"It's *not* your project," he growled, cutting her off. "It's GAO's. And it's up to them to decide who's best equipped to lead such a delicate mission."

"And you're the one best equipped?"

He could swear she choked on her tongue at the unintended *double-entendre*. As if she were still the virgin who'd dissolved in his arms for those long, delirious months. She must have garnered experience since him.

Since him? Ha. By the time she'd left him, she could have given advanced courses to the most notorious *femme fatale*.

He pressed closer. "I am. Want a reminder?"

A flush swept her face. "Spare me, Roque." She struggled with what looked like a dozen rants all demanding to erupt at once. Then one won, spilled from her flushed lips in a hot gush. "Just what the hell do you mean, 'concerns about the nature and purpose of the documentary'? This is the first I've heard of any such nonsense. Though it wasn't my idea, when I was approached for it, I thought it a great one. Those endangered people need to have their story told with compassion and realism, to raise awareness of their plight."

He smirked. "As I said, a worthy cause. One that is sure to catapult you to unparalleled fame."

"This is not about me! This has nothing to do with me!"

"It doesn't? You won't star in this 'documentary'?"

"Star? Where *are* you getting these ridiculous ideas?"

"You're not going to be the narrator, the viewer's guide to this exotic world and the heart-wrenching human drama?"

This gave her pause. At length, she nodded. "They did ask

me to appear with my team in a few shots while we performed our duties. Is this why…?" She stopped again. "Listen, I've seen samples of the production company's documentaries and they were certainly no commercial fluff. I don't know where GAO got the idea that…" Her eyes widened on incensed realization. "It was you! You planted this idea that this was some sort of maneuver to exploit the expedition for commercial ends!"

"I didn't plant anything. I just made information available to them. That the director of your film crew works mainly on commercials and reality shows, who you really are and what you once did for a living. They drew their own conclusions."

"So *that's* how you made them give you the reins of the expedition!"

He shrugged again. "Giving them to me was the least they could do, considering I'm the one financing the whole thing."

Some new word had to be invented for what filled her eyes. Shock was too mild a word. He had expected this piece of information to surprise her, but to that extent?

He watched her struggle with her out-of-control distress, if only for moments. Then it was his turn to be surprised at the disdain flooding in its wake, the knowing gleam entering her eyes. "As the expedition is costing almost a million dollars, you must have married an heiress somewhere along the way."

So she really didn't know. Hadn't bothered to find out.

He pressed her backwards until she was flush against the truck's side. He *was* going to enjoy this.

He smiled his spite down on her. "Now, how could I marry an heiress when I'm still married to you, *minha esposa?*"

CHAPTER FOUR

"YOU'RE *not* still married to me!"

Jewel heard the croaking whisper. It was hers. It hung there in the air, swirling with his words. His impossible words.

They're not impossible, moron, a furious inner voice spat.

She hadn't divorced him. To leave him the chance to come out of their mess of a marriage with what he'd wanted. She'd felt she'd owed him for all the pleasure and passion, no matter his reasons for giving them to her. The pain she'd invited, marrying him knowing he hadn't wanted her for herself.

But when Immigration hadn't contacted her to confirm the validity of their marriage, she'd assumed Roque had abandoned his plans to obtain American citizenship through her. She'd been sure he'd divorced her, had taken his pick of the endless women who clamored for him and had carried on with his plans without her.

So what did he mean?

"You're not still married to me!" she choked again, a ridiculous conviction possessing her that if she said it enough, it would go away.

Black amusement lit his eyes. "Your horror is a mortal

blow, *amor.*" He clicked his tongue lazily. "Is this any way to react to the jubilant fact that I'm still your husband?"

"You're *not* my husband!"

"First, I'm not your leader—and we know how that debate ended—and now I'm not your husband. Anything else I'm not?"

"Yes! You're not qualified to lead this expedition."

"I beg to differ, *meu doce.* I am a surgeon with an extensive experience in thoracic, trauma, minimally invasive, video and computer-assisted surgery—and I won't even list the rest of my areas of expertise. While you are just an internist."

He'd hit on the one sure way to eradicate her horror and resurrect her fury. The sheer gall of his snobbery!

It must be another addition to his character. He hadn't had it in him before. At least, he'd never bared it to her when he'd needed to be on her good side. Or maybe he'd been in no position to flaunt a non-existent superiority. He sure was flaunting it now he had it.

"*Just* an internist?" she fumed.

His nod was pure condescension. "*Sim,* and barely one, too. You started late in this doctoring business, *amor.*"

So she'd started her medical education at twenty-two, changing her life's course—starting over, really. She'd just finished her residency, but she'd had it through GAO's unorthodox medical licensing program, gotten her training in the field and in trials by fire. Her skills covered a wide range and her experience level rivaled that of veteran doctors in generic career paths. If he knew anything about GAO's standards, he'd know that. Dammit, he'd just seen her in action, seen her standards for himself. It seemed he wasn't much impressed.

"And that makes me, what? Inferior?" she spat.

His tone grew even more patronizing. "No, it makes you a great sidekick."

The urge to punch his imposing nose was almost unbearable. "Watch you don't get a great side-kick in the teeth, buster."

Ridiculously thick lashes jolted up, unguarded eyes fired emerald. Then he threw his magnificent head back and laughed.

"Ah, *Jóia*." He wiped away tears of laughter with both hands, deep chuckles still rumbling in his chest like distant thunder. "This is going to be far more pleasurable than I anticipated."

"*This* is going to end right now, Roque. For the expedition's sake. If you think the next eight weeks are going to be anything like the stuff you're used to…"

Steel slashed in his eyes, cutting her off. "And you know what 'stuff' I'm used to, *Jóia*? Do you know *anything* about me?"

No, I don't. The retort almost erupted from her.

And her self-enforced ignorance had started when they'd first met. In trying to escape his pursuit, his influence, to cling to her commitment to Michael, she'd thought the less she'd known about Roque, the more she could resist him. Apart from her very favorable—and as suspect as her psychological state at the time—observations, there'd only been condemnation volunteered by others. Not that it had stopped her from succumbing to his seduction. She'd married him without confronting him, deciding to remain in the dark, afraid to discover evidence to validate the condemnation and her insecurities.

But she wasn't about to tell him that. She raised her chin, gave him her best belittling look. "I know enough."

"Really? Beyond my name, age and profession, what more did you care to find out about me before we got married?"

His intensity shook her, made her blurt out defensively, "I knew everything I needed to know. I knew you were concluding your post-graduate studies while working—"

"In the hospital where your vaunted ex-fiancé was the

director and your father was a major shareholder," he completed for her in a totally bored tone. "That's common knowledge, nothing a wife could state as privileged information about her husband."

Oh, she knew more. Revealing, disturbing tidbits supplied by his myriad friends, competitors—and women. That he had no family, had lived close to the poverty line most of his life, had had a temporary U.S. visa he'd needed to make permanent. Heading all had been insights into why he'd pursued her, married her. And it hadn't been because he'd loved and wanted her, as he'd sworn.

He took her glare to mean she was stymied. His lips twisted. "You certainly have no idea what 'stuff' I'm used to."

"So what? What I don't know I can guess with reliable accuracy. At least in this matter. Hospital surgeons are a different breed from field ones. I don't need any specific knowledge of you to know surgeons like you depend on ordered schedules and everything at your fingertips in highly equipped ORs, with legions of personnel as one buffer after another between you and the immediacy of your patients' needs."

The last flicker of lightness left his eyes. She had to forcibly stop herself from cringing.

"So you don't know anything about me," he drawled, grim, almost frightening. "And you've just seen me in a field procedure, and yet you still presume to say 'surgeons like you'. Has your mother never taught you what a bad girl presumptions and prejudices make you, *minha esposa?*"

A twinge ran down her chest, stopped her breathing.

When she finally spoke, her voice sounded distant in her ears, clinical even. "I thought you knew my mother was never around to teach me anything, wasn't even around after my hit and run, too horrified that the perfect daughter she boasted about was broken. I haven't seen her in longer than I've seen you, not since she found a reason to cut me off completely when I left her choice of a socially compatible groom and married you. Thanks for the kind reminder, though. But just in case you think you've rubbed salt into my wounds, don't. I would give anything to be able to feel pain at her absence from my life, to miss her, to think of her with anything besides resignation."

His bronze face turned dark copper. With anger? No. It looked more like…mortification?

Oh, come on! Why should he be mortified, thinking that he'd hurt her, when it had been his intention to do just that?

But it did seem like she'd read his reaction right. His next words were proof enough. "*Jóia, perdoe-me,* I *was* being spiteful. I know how negligent your mother was, how it affected you, especially after your accident. And no matter what, I don't hurt others, wouldn't hurt you, this way. Ever. I'm sorry."

She stared. He was sorry? For hurting her? When he was here for what seemed to be the sole purpose of doing just that?

She exhaled, shook her head. "As I said, it didn't hurt."

She stopped as she realized. It did.

But it hadn't been his dig into her non-existent relationship with her mother that had hurt. It was him poking an accusing finger at a practice she loathed and was guilty of, and her acute sense of fairness lashing her in response.

She'd seen how he'd operated outside the stereotyped medium she'd just painted. Even if she didn't believe he could do that on a regular basis, she abhorred generalizations, knew from firsthand trauma how blithe bias hurt and damaged. She never inflicted either on another.

But this was Roque. The man who'd once tried to exploit her.

The man who was now usurping her role in her most important endeavor ever. Who was as good as accusing her of being self-serving and fame-hungry! She owed him no apologies.

Her conscience still prodded her to give it a go anyway. "Listen, Roque, all I was saying is, if you are really coming, you should leave the work to me and enjoy the scenery aboard our riverboat until a case that requires your talents comes along. Leading this expedition requires familiarity with the objectives and logistical versatility, not surgical prowess. Only I, who have been involved from day one, can provide that."

He shrugged one daunting shoulder. "Then you'll come in handy dealing with the logistical side, freeing me to take care of the medical one. You're good but you can't be experienced enough for a mission this complex and unpredictable."

"You have no idea how experienced I am!" OK, so that came out way different from what she'd intended.

And it was no surprise when he didn't let the opportunity pass. "And I can't wait to find out, *encantador.*"

"Quit with the innuendos already! So what if you financed this? I don't see every expedition financier trotting out to join it, and getting in experienced people's way."

"You realize the more you talk about your 'experience', the more imperative it becomes for me to sample it, don't you?"

"Stop word-twisting! I don't know where you got enough money to throw a million of it around, and I don't *want* to know, but you can't buy your way into this!"

"Weird, because I did buy all of this, period. You wouldn't have an expedition if I hadn't subsidized it, *minha esposa.*"

"Stop calling me that! I'm not your wife. I was never your wife. And we both know it."

"You might have known it, but I surely wasn't in on that little secret. I was so deluded I thought you were my wife, for better or for worse. The delusion still persists to this moment. Along with all the binding legal documents, *meu doce.*"

Binding legal documents. Surely he wouldn't lie about something like this? Not when she could easily check? This was real then. They *were* still married.

Oh, God!

But why hadn't he divorced her? And, most important: "Why are you doing this? Why did you fabricate this *farce* about reality shows to smear me to GAO? Is this your revenge?"

He raised both eyebrows. "Why should I want revenge?"

"I don't know!" And she didn't. Wanting revenge indicated being hurt. He had to have cared for her for real to be hurt.

He went on, in that reasonable tone that made her want to scream, "And don't you think if I'd wanted revenge I would have sought it long before now? And, anyway, how can it be revenge if you're not harboring any self-serving intentions and my presence here won't spoil any of your plans?"

"I have no plans!" she almost screamed.

"In that case, why are you all up in arms? Why don't you just accept that I'm here to supervise this, to regulate you…"

"I don't need to be regulated! I can't believe GAO believed this rubbish, let you do this to me!"

"What am I doing? I'm here to work, and to see you."

Yeah. Right. "Well, I don't want to see you. Not in this life, not in the next."

He whistled, impressed this time. "Really? Hard to understand your angst when it was you who walked out on me. And not at all nicely, *meu bela.*"

She felt sore and swollen, as if she'd been ramming her body against jagged, unyielding rock. She shouldn't be surprised. She already knew how intractable he was when he latched onto an objective. She tried one last time. "Why don't you go away, Roque? Just go away and leave me to get on with my work."

His gaze shifted away from her. Hers followed and she only then realized they were back at the pier. The sun was setting. And then the tropical rain started falling, sudden, steady, shrouding.

He was unperturbed at being drenched in seconds, as was she. But she was used to the daily showers. He only gestured towards Rio Solimões, the Amazon River in the region. "See this great river, *amor?* My going away is as probable as getting to ice-skate on its surface. I'm here to stay, *Jóia.* Get over it."

Her heart stampeded, her eyeballs heated. Would she burst with frustration? She glared her resentment at him as the clanking vehicle slowed down. The moment it came to a coughing halt, she erupted to her feet—and the sunset disappeared.

The lights came back in moments. She was in Roque's arms. She'd blacked out. Must have been caused by standing up so suddenly.

"Close your eyes, *bela.* I'll carry you to your cabin." His lips moved on her temple and his voice penetrated her brain.

She jolted out of his arms, fought the imbalance and disorientation, tried to rise to her knees. An aggravated sound spilled from him as he rose, jumped out of the truck. Then he reached up for her. Still groggy, she instinctively reached down and he took her in his arms. This time he kept her there.

"Put me down, Roque." Her eyes darted around when he just looked down on her and smiled, ignoring her demand. Madeline and Inácio were pretending not to notice as they followed. What must they be thinking now? After her painstakingly established record for detachment and lack of interest in men?

Nothing worse than the truth, that was for sure.

The locals had no such qualms, had no intention of missing out on Roque's displays, watching openly. There went the take-charge, professional image she'd meticulously constructed!

"Put me down if you want to keep your teeth, Roque."

"You'd ram them and risk teeth marks on that perfect forehead? After all the trouble you went to, to make it so?"

A twinge lanced through her. He thought her desire to look whole again, what? Frivolous? He could talk. He'd certainly never known what it meant to be reviled and discarded because he'd ceased to look pleasing.

He suddenly grimaced, put her down, slowly, carefully, but his embrace didn't even loosen. If she had to get out of it, she had to give their audience a fight scene. No point risking the last of her authority-figure tatters when she was sure he'd end up winning one way or another. But it wasn't that that enraged her. It was the tremors of pleasure shooting through her from every point of contact with every hard inch of him. Her mind might be averse but her body recognized its mate, clamored for him.

No, he wasn't her mate any more! Would never be again.

She pushed at him, refusing to be a pawn in whatever game he was playing. He let her go at last and she staggered around on elastic legs.

He fell into step with her, caught her hand, pressed it, an entreaty not to snatch it away. An entreaty? Hah!

"Jewel—again, I'm sorry. That last crack—it was stupid and cruel the way it came out. I didn't mean it. I just wanted to take you to your cabin. You were barely standing by the time the tribe let us go. I would have insisted on handling the emergency alone if I'd known you've been pushing it, sleeping four hours maximum for the last four days, working non-stop loading the boats since two a.m...." She snapped a look at him and he sighed. "*Sim,* Madeline and Inácio told me."

"You questioned them? When?" She snapped her head back, stared ahead, waved her hand. "Oh, I know when. The first moment you got them alone during the village's feast, right? And I'm sure you volunteered information in return."

"Like the fact that I'm your estranged husband? I sure did. Or did you prefer them to think that you and a man you just met can be all over each other like we've been?"

"I wasn't…" She fell silent, fighting a charring wave of anger. No use. Anything she'd do or say now, she'd end up losing more. Let him play caveman. Or, rather, a huge, majestic cat, leisurely playing with his kill, drawing out its torment for laughs. There was one way out of this. She had to take it.

She did. "Fine, Roque, you win."

His uncanny eyes flared. Triumphant, was he? She wondered how he'd feel when he realized how total his victory was.

His arm snaked around her waist, gathering her to him, something soft entering his gaze. Soft? Sure.

She lurched a step backward and out of his hold, snarled her admission of defeat. "You win. And you stay. I'm leaving."

CHAPTER FIVE

ROQUE watched Jewel walk away.

It seemed all he did was watch her walk away.

And though he knew he should let her go this time, should consider he'd won, had achieved his mission, he couldn't. All he knew was that he was damned if he'd let her walk away again. This time anyone doing the walking away would be him.

He followed her, his steps slow, his thoughts racing, scalding emotions roaring in his system. He could name them very well now. Anger, aggravation, arousal.

He watched her tall, lithe figure reach the row of boats docked at the pier, climb onto the lower deck of the triple-deck, steel-hulled riverboat he'd picked for this expedition. If only she knew how much more money over her estimated million he'd poured into that selection.

He'd had the boat almost rebuilt, not only for this mission but for what he intended to be a regular endeavor, reaching out to the isolated, endangered people of his country. He'd made sure it would be sturdy enough to withstand the rigors of constant use by replacing the hull and engine, and that it would rival a luxury cruise boat by having installed air-conditioning in all cabins and public-use areas and fitting each cabin in cedar and Amazon mahogany and private baths and showers. He wanted the humanitarian workers who'd use it to know how their efforts were appreciated, to give them much-deserved comforts.

He'd picked this boat after reviewing dozens of Amazon-faring riverboats because it was the only one that had a suite, separate from the rest of the accommodation, occupying the fore of the third deck with its own covered and uncovered sundecks. He'd planned to have it himself, for keeping apart from the rest of his colleagues. From her. That no longer appealed. The only thing that did appeal now was for her to share it with him. But he had to keep her here first.

He bounded the steps onto the lower deck, followed the trace of soap and woman and clean sweat. Her unique scent. It maddened further, quickened his stomping impatience to the cabin, where it intensified. He shoved the door open.

His heart swelled with stimulation when she whirled up from her bent pose over an open suitcase. A thrill coursed down his spine as she snarled, "Get out, Roque."

"No." He advanced into the cabin, clearing one bed, snatching the suitcase out of her reach. "I'm not getting out. And neither are you." Then he took her by the shoulders.

He'd intended to tell her she wasn't backing out now that she wasn't getting her way, was seeing this through, *his* way.

Then she filled his hands and everything that had happened since she'd left him ceased to matter. Nothing existed but her stunned eyes confessing equal awareness, her flesh humming with their resurrected affinity, her gasping breath filling his lungs with an overdose of the scent he'd homed in on. And now he had to have the taste.

He bent to get it and she stumbled backwards, lost her balance, grabbed his arms involuntarily, and missed.

He caught at her tumbling body and it dragged him down, plummeting them both to the carpeted deck. He managed to twist before they hit it, cushioning her. He lay beneath her until their momentum was spent. Then he tumbled her around.

Deus, he'd missed her feel beneath him. He'd craved it, burned for it. He let all the savoring out in a long, ragged groan, wallowing in the turbulent deadlock of their gazes, the fusion of their panting breaths. Then her lips moved, mouthing his name. There was only so much he could stand.

He took his unuttered name from her lips, and they both jolted at the contact. So it was still the same, the shock to the system any level of intimacy with her elicited. The addictive reaction nothing and no one else had ever come close to imitating. He went after more, glided against her moist softness, probed then plunged, strained to drain her of each breath and sound that lay unformed deep within her.

He growled for her reciprocation, and as if his fierceness ignited hers, she opened for him, took his tongue, buried him in her response, in her scorching velvet and taste.

And it was ten years ago again, at that New Year's Eve party, before her accident, when he'd made his first pre-emptive strike to sever her existing tie and claim her for himself. He renewed his onslaught now, the need to recapture her roaring in his blood, no thoughts of holding back like that first time.

He hardened beyond agony, simulating the ultimate intimacy they'd once perfected. His hands ran in a frenzy of memory over her hair, her face, melting down her neck to her breasts. He wrenched his mouth away and she moaned. He met her eyes, dimly realized he must look exactly like that. Delirious, *in extremis.* They'd always driven each other to incoherence.

And she'd been able to walk out on him. To have enough of him. She'd been able to stay away. For eight years.

She couldn't stay away for eight heartbeats now, whimpering with the few seconds' deprivation. Her hands flailed the urgent worshipping that had once made him believe she'd felt the same, running down his back, convulsing on his hips, dragging them to her core, as she, too, shook in the grip of the brutal need for satisfaction.

He'd satisfy her. He'd satisfy her until she begged for the pleasure to end, to never end. He had eight years to make up for. Right now, later tonight—all through the whole expedition—would only make up for the first few hours of her desertion.

He yanked off his vest, tore open his wet shirt, clawed at her rain-plastered one.

He longed to slide down her body, wallow in the tormenting ecstasy of unhindered contact. Then, when he'd hoarded enough pleas, he'd bend over her, sweep his tongue along the scar that snaked from her left pubic bone, across her midriff, below her left breast, fading to nothing in her armpit. Only when he had her weeping in arousal, he'd take pity on her, on himself, and thrust inside her…

Shaking, his every tremor resonating in her body, he fumbled to undo her bra and she arched up to help him. He growled deep in anticipation as he rose to look full on her exposed beauty—and everything inside him stilled. There was no scar!

Breath emptied out of him on a jolt of horror. It was as if he'd woken up in mid-trance to find himself making love to a stranger. Then realization hit him like a punch in the gut.

She'd had *whole-body* scar revisions, not only facial.

This was what her body had been like before the accident. Only better. Time and nature had imbued it with a feminine ripeness that sent his every male fiber into distress. He wanted her now—*now,* hard and fast and agonizingly satisfying.

But he felt her stiffening, passion draining from her hands and eyes, self-revulsion and fury replacing them. His shock had lasted for heartbeats, but it had shocked her, too, back to the reality of their estrangement and conflict.

She pushed at him. "Get off me, Roque."

He pressed harder into her. "Don't even think of going cold on me now, not after I've felt you, felt what you feel. If you're thinking it's wrong or too soon, let me put you straight. It's not wrong and it's eight years too damn late, *amor.* Let me—"

"You don't need this." Her rasp was as painful as a dull knife cutting through his words and thoughts. "If my absence is holding up your American citizenship procedures, just say so."

Roque stared down at her, for what felt like an hour.

Then, in measured movements, he removed his body from hers and she scrambled away, struggled to put her clothes back in order, to suppress the pangs racking her flesh at losing contact with his.

He unfolded to his full height, still staring at her, making no effort to button his shirt. She kept her burning eyes on his face, watched a black frown forming there. Was he upset that she'd worked it out?

She hadn't. Others had worked it out for her. They'd said that as a rich, broken innocent who'd been discarded by all, starting with her parents and glamorous milieu and ending with the appearance-obsessed modeling world, with only Michael wanting her still, for her parents' connections, she'd been the perfect means to all of Roque's ends. The one stone with which to take his revenge on Michael for depriving him of a lucrative position, to get that position, money and a Green Card.

But she'd never confronted him over these allegations, had decided not to listen to anyone, letting time tell her the truth.

But time, compounded by their soaring passion and his too wonderful, too careful, too *calculated* treatment of her, had only compounded her insecurity. She sometimes thought she might have overcome it all, even come to accept his motivations in marrying her, until she'd discovered what would have ended even a healthy marriage. After her miscarriage she would have done anything to end it. She *had* said anything to make it end.

But even in their last explosive scene, the citizenship issue hadn't come up. She'd hurled far-fetched insults at him, not her real suspicions, to get him to let her go.

Now she just wanted him to stop scowling and answer her!

His scowl dissolved, but he still didn't answer. Instead, a huff escaped him. Then another. Then he burst out laughing.

She endured a whole minute before she snarled, "Laugh any more and I'll probably have to intubate and ventilate you!"

He began to choke. She circled him, thumped him between his shoulder blades. His laughing fit sputtered to a coughing one.

She smirked. "You can now thank me for saving your life."

He wiped his tears, still rumbling raspy chuckles that abraded her, as if her nerves lay over her skin. "You probably have. You should issue alerts before dishing out something like that. I never dreamed you were funny, *Jóia.*" Then his chuckles died out. "Or at least you would have been if this was a joke. But it isn't, is it? You actually believe I want American citizenship? What for? I never had any intention of living anywhere but in Brazil. And I was always welcome in the States or anywhere else, even before I became an entrepreneur."

"A *what?*"

Roque felt oppression fisting around his heart at her incredulity. At the new blow she'd dealt him.

Compared to the user he'd just found out she'd thought

him, the gigolo she'd once made him feel like sounded good. At least a gigolo was honest about his motivations, rendered an agreed-upon service.

He attempted another chuckle. It grazed him on the way out. "You never heard of the innovations I made to diagnostic equipment and procedures?" He gave a sarcastic snort at her widening gape. "*Sim*, contrary to your belief that I married an heiress and milked her dry, I actually got my fortune the legitimate way. The patents alone were bought for half a billion dollars by a medical appliances conglomerate. And I get paid *very* big money every time I tutor surgeons around the world."

He watched his words hitting her, felt her grappling with his revelations and felt something inside him snap.

That was so unbelievable to her? She'd thought him incapable of succeeding on his own? Was that why she hadn't divorced him? She'd been leaving him the opportunity to acquire the prized American citizenship she was sure he must crave to help him out? How *generous* of her.

And meantime, what had she used her marital staus for? Kept it secret, going by Dr. Johansson, then divulged it only as a deterrent when men wanted more? He wondered how many more men she'd devastated then abandoned.

Jewel watched Roque's face hardening into a mask of wrath that again almost had her cringing.

Feeling small and foolish, she decided to just get it over with. She exhaled. "So you're a business mogul now. What are you doing here, then? With your new clout, if you thought I was turning this expedition into a reality show, you could have just taken me off the roster, replaced me with whomever you thought suitable from among the hordes who now, no doubt, answer to you. You didn't have to come here yourself."

"Contrary to what you're implying," he ground out, "I never wanted to become a doctor to amass power and fortune. But they have come in handy, made me able to do my job on a far-reaching scale. And though you make it sound as if I sit in my rarefied medium, being waited on, field missions have always been an integral part of my schedule. The only difference is that for the past five years I've been able to finance as many as I like. They also have another advantage, they make me a far more effective doctor. After the energy drain in ORs, labs and meetings, being out in the open and out of the system for good chunks of time, reaching the people I became a doctor to serve is the best anti-burnout measure there is. And this is another such mission."

Jewel had heard that same fervor before. When he'd spoken of his vocation, of what people with abilities and privileges owed the world. Back then she'd thought it had been part of his technique for landing gullible girls. Even then, it had left her with a growing dissatisfaction with her whole life, had been the catalyst that had made her start over after she'd left him.

It seemed it hadn't been a line.

"As to why I picked this specific mission from the dozens I could have financed and joined, I already told you."

"Yeah, to stop me from turning the expedition into a launching pad for my new career in reality shows. What do you think I would do after that? Go back to modeling? Or go on to a Hollywood acting career?"

He shrugged his indifference.

So. That was it, then. Why he was here. What he was now.

And that was what she was now. A hypocrite. She *had* been harboring an inane, insane wish that he was here for *her.* Even if for the ulterior motives she'd thought he had. Pathetic.

But even if those motives *had* been valid once, they were

a thing of the past now he was far richer than both her parents combined. Now she'd better put this in the past, too.

She gave him her best effort at a smile. "Seems you had a meteoric rise. Very impressive, Roque. Congratulations. I hope you have all the recharging you need on this mission and that it won't be a bother when I leave you with no second in command."

With that she turned to the door, held it open for him. He put on his vest, prowled towards her, potent vibes she couldn't begin to guess at blasting off him.

He took the door from her, pushed it wider until it clunked on the wall. Then he pressed her against it, imprinting her with every hard inch of himself. His gaze burned down on her, as if waiting for something. The shudder that shook her was it, it seemed.

At feeling it, his eyes fired, then one hand glided over her, from ribcage to breast to neck before melting to the back of her head. The other took the same journey downwards to cup her buttocks. He leisurely spread her unresisting body for a fierce thrust of arousal at her core, then, holding her eyes, absorbing every shocked tremor of pleasure streaking through her, quivering all over her face, he devoured her.

When her whimpers became incessant, when she was devouring him back, he slowly, too slowly, unfused their mouths and bodies, a cruel twist to his lips.

Then he turned around and walked away.

Before he went out of hearing range he tossed back a dark drawl. "As I said before, *minha esposa,* you're going nowhere."

She stood plastered to the door until someone passed by and asked if she was sick. She shook her head, closed the door with a measured click. Then she stumbled to her bed, fell on it face down, shame and humiliation, hunger and anger suffocating her.

He could have dragged her to bed and she would have begged him to hurry, as she always had, disintegrating with the unbearable need for his invasion, his completion.

But he'd walked out. Right after he'd made both of them sure that he could have had her if he'd wanted. And he hadn't.

So why did he want her to stay? Not that he'd said he wanted her to stay, he'd *told* her she was staying. To what end? Now she knew his reasons for being here, she understood the cat-and-mouse game he'd been playing with her so far even less. But when had she ever understood him, or his motives…?

Roque felt rage entering the danger zone as he stomped up to his cabin. The humidity-soaked air only contributed to his spiking temperature.

Once he'd burst inside, he yanked his clothes off then stepped out on the aft sundeck, raised his eyes to the sky. Against a backdrop of blackness, the uncanny stars of Amazonia crowded in a random pattern of steadily gleaming jewels…jewels…

With a growl, he hauled himself up on the railing. He stood balanced for a moment, then he dove.

He cut the water surface in a clean slice, hurtled downward with the momentum of his thirty-foot dive. It felt like plunging into black ink, into a sense-distorting dimension.

He stopped descending, maneuvered himself upright and remained suspended in the depths for long, unearthly moments. When his lungs began to burn, he kicked his way to the surface.

He took a few deep breaths then swam out into the river, the gentle current boosting his crawl. The river was thirty miles wide here, making seeing its other bank hard even during the day. Now it felt like swimming into a void. That suited him fine right now.

With his thoughts slowing down, he did too, floated, let the current sweep him along. His unseeing eyes fixed on the starry dome as his inner vision crowded with memories. With her. Jewel. His precious, flawed Jewel who'd repolished herself, remolded and reinvented herself.

He had to admit it, turning from a model into a doctor, and the skilled one he'd seen, had been a staggering leap. Undertaking humanitarian missions, no matter how self-serving the end, was as big. She'd achieved unimaginable growth in many areas.

And she'd thought he'd married her to use her. And though it made him want to shake her until her every bone rattled, he could see where her suspicions had come from, how they had polluted her view of his character, fueled her distance and aloofness, and led to that final mutilating showdown.

Now, as anger ebbed, premeditation, which had seen him through his meteoric rise, as she'd called it, which had made him certain of his abilities and dead set on his goals, settled in.

His goals… Right now he could only see one. Jewel. Working beside him, dueling with him, walking away from him, shuddering in his arms, on the floor, against the door…

Fire flooded his veins again. So even the Amazon River wasn't enough to douse it.

But he didn't want it doused. Now the past had been put in perspective, only one thing mattered. He still wanted her. Badly.

And she wanted him, too. No doubt about it. But this time the last thing he wanted was ever-afters. They may still be legally married, but all he wanted was an all-out affair, to purge the accumulated hunger. Once it had been, he'd be free at last.

The boat was now a tiny twinkle in the distance. He swept around, started the vigorous swim back, smiling all the way.

CHAPTER SIX

"GIVEN up on trying to sleep, *minha esposa?*"

The mocking words hit Jewel in the spine as she hastily retreated from the dining hall's entrance.

She hadn't made a sound. And he'd been facing away from the door. Talk about eyes in the back of his head. But just how had he known it had been her? And what was he doing here at this hour? She'd thought she'd be the only one here at 4:00 a.m.

Well, she wasn't and she should walk back in and get her breakfast. She had a long day ahead of her and the sooner she was done the better. She turned, re-entered the hall, headed for the open-plan kitchen. There were no meals served at this hour. She'd make her own.

She circled as far away from him as possible, making every effort to keep her eyes off him. She still felt him rising from his chair, following her. And not because he made any sound.

"Having trouble sleeping, too?" She took her cue from him, asking the nonchalant question.

"With you around?" Lazy yet heated teasing permeated his voice. "Do you even need to ask? But you really have to do something about your attitude, *Jóia*. It won't inspire team co-operation if you leave every room I'm in."

She opened the refrigerator. "Have you had breakfast?"

A moment of silence stretched in answer. From the way her senses were going haywire, she could tell he was now no more than a foot away. She kept her eyes on her chore.

He finally drawled, "At four a.m.? Hardly. Are you offering me some? That would be a first."

And he was right about that. During their five-month marriage, she'd never fed him anything. Besides the dazed state in which she'd spent those months, she hadn't even mastered boiling water. He'd cooked when he hadn't brought takeaway coming home from work. He'd been handy with fast and simple yet delicious meals.

"And it would be a last, so enjoy it while you can," she tossed over her shoulder. "You like omelets?"

"Doesn't everybody? And why, pray tell, would this un-precedented occasion be an unrepeatable one?"

She placed the pan on the stove, got out a bowl to mix her ingredients. "Simple. As I already told you, I'm leaving. I doubt I'll see you again."

"Ah, that again. Another thing you really have to work on—this new habit of repeating yourself, *amor*." His hands landed on her shoulder. When had he moved? Good thing she'd already put the eggs down. "Give me one good reason why you should leave."

She shook her shoulders, and his hands dropped. "You."

His hands were back on her instantly, turning her to face him. And he was naked!

Breathe. He *wasn't* naked. Only down his wide-open shirt to his very, very low-hanging jeans waistband.

She remembered his every muscle and sinew. This was way

more. He must have found time to upgrade his body among his preoccupations. Those field missions must have been rigorous, too. Her hands itched, her mouth watered. Oh, great. She was dying to grab at him, was drooling over him now.

She had to get out of here fast.

He waited for her stunned eyes to rise to his again then gave a mind-messing whisper. "Nice to know I'm a good reason."

"The best," she rasped.

Something primal rumbled in his gut as he closed the space between them, pressing her to the kitchen counter. "Jewel…"

Her hands flattened on each satin-steel pectoralis, virtually sizzled on contact. "Roque, this stopped being funny a while ago."

He covered her hands with his. "You mean it was funny to start with? That wasn't my impression."

"If it wasn't funny, then you gave a very good simulation of enjoying yourself at my expense."

"I'd rather enjoy myself *with* you, *Jóia.*"

She snatched her tingling hands away, pushed out of his grip. "Drop this seduction act. You've graciously explained why you're here. And you've already achieved your purpose. You've driven the wannabe reality show starlet away."

"If this isn't what you had planned, stay and prove it."

"I don't have to prove anything to you and I'm not staying where my intentions are maligned and my authority is ridiculed. So—a full year's work is down the drain and I'm out of here to start something else, somewhere else from scratch. Your mission is accomplished. What more do you want?"

"Certainly not money or a Green Card."

"OK, be cryptic." He chuckled and reached for her again. She dodged him, her heart tottering inside her chest. "But do it sitting down or there won't be any omelets."

He caught her back again, growled in her nape, "Damn food. I want *you*. That's exactly what I want. All of you."

It wasn't only an admission of need but a declaration of intent, a bolt of lightning emptying her lungs, her mind. She choked, "You want a woman you think so unethical, so inhumane she'd exploit others' suffering to gain fame and fortune?"

He turned her around, his lips and words on her neck, branding her. "When was I ever able to care about the drawbacks where you're concerned? I'd disregard any qualm, risk any consequence, pay any price, to have you."

Each rasp and meaning speared through her heart, sank into her breasts and loins. She throbbed all over with an escalating ache. She pushed at him. "How flattering. Excuse me if I don't want a man who wants me when he thinks the worst of me."

"*You* wanted *me* when you evidently thought the worst of me. You wanted me with every breath for five months." She lurched at his reminder, its brutal truth, at the memory of the clawing, perpetual need that had been forced into dormancy in the past years and had now been resurrected, as urgent, as tormenting. More. His hands ran up her back, infusing her with tension. "You want me again now."

It was pointless to deny it. She leaned back in the circle of his arms and gasped, "I want to jump out of a plane without a parachute, too. You won't see me succumbing to that desire either."

He rubbed against her with a satisfied chuckle, let her feel the hard promise of endless pleasure. "I'm that dangerous?"

"More." There was no chance she'd jump out of a plane. There was every chance she would succumb in his arms. And she wouldn't survive another such episode of sheer lunacy.

She pushed away again and suddenly he let her go. She stumbled around, picked up the knife, put it down again. The way she was trembling she'd slice her fingers and not the onion. She turned to the less dangerous side of omelet-making, whipping eggs, adding herbs and spices. Just as she thought they'd have to settle for a plain omelet, he came up behind her, snaked his arms around her waist—and picked up the knife and cutting board.

She swayed back to the fridge, got out butter, put it in the pan to melt, all the time snatching sideway glances at his hands as he proceeded to chop. Rapid, precise, practiced, producing heaps of even cubes and slices of onions, tomatoes and mushrooms. It figured. Those were the surgeon's hands that had made him rich and famous, that had once made her—

Stop! Don't go there now. Or ever.

He handed her the heaped board, then leaned back on the counter to watch her. Her hands trembled as she slid the onion and tomato in the pan first, and hot butter splashed her.

A smothered gasp tore out of her as her hands snapped up to shield her face. Roque jumped at her, dragged her away to the sink, feverish eyes roving her for burn marks.

"It's nothing," she gasped. "A tiny splatter hit my neck."

Urgent hands pushed her hair back, tipped her chin and examined her neck. Then his tension drained. He must have found nothing alarming. He still wet his hand and wiped cool water on the sting, over and over. Then he bent, opened his mouth on it and licked, gentle, insistent. The sting disappeared, to be replaced by a blistering torrent engulfing her whole body.

"Better?" The murmur spread on his soothing tongue, vibrated in her flesh. It couldn't be worse! All she could do was nod.

In silence, she finished making the omelet while he readied plates and toast. Then he took the pan from her, filled their plates, picked them up and gestured for her to lead the way to a table.

Stiff footsteps took her to the nearest table. He put down the plates and hurried to pull a chair back for her. After seating her, he pulled a chair as near as possible to her and sat down.

He sniffed the aroma rising from his plate. *"Divino."* He sampled a fork and groaned, *"Delicioso."* Then he attacked the rest with evident enjoyment.

Pleasure coursed through her at his praise. So she hankered for his approval now? Was there no end to her folly?

For God's sake, just eat.

To her surprise, she was starving and she demolished her plate just moments after he had his.

He gave a satisfied sigh as he leaned back and patted his flat, muscled abdomen. "That was magnificent, *amor.*"

Heat rose in her cheeks. "It was just an omelet."

He gave her a complacent glance. "There is no such thing as *just* anything. In the wrong hands anything can be a disaster. In the right ones everything can become a masterpiece."

Her heat shot off the scale. "Quit flattering me, Roque."

"I never flatter, you or anyone else. With me you get the truth and nothing but the truth."

She harumphed. "The truth according to you, of course."

"The truth is mostly point of view, *amor,* and I'm never rigid about mine. But I never say what I don't mean, whether it's praise or criticism. I think since yesterday I already proved that I'm not averse to saying what I think to your face, no matter how unfavorable. Though in such conditions I'm always open to being proved wrong. As for favorable things, I meant—and mean—every word. Every last one."

Oh. "Well, you did half the work."

He gave a dismissive pout. "I just chopped raw ingredients.

I didn't concoct that elusive seasoning, didn't cook each in-gredient to the exact degree to make the result perfect." Gentle fingers brushed her feverish cheek. "So you've been hiding your culinary talents from me."

"I picked them up under duress…" She swallowed, forced her voice to steady. "My first field mission was long and I was in danger of starving with our cook's version of food napalm."

He laughed, a deep melody that spread things she'd never had with him inside her. Ease. Fun. Companionship. That was weirder than anything that had gone on before.

His hand cupped her face, his smile pouring right into her heart. "Survival is a great teacher. In your case, a superlative one. I can't wait to sample a more complex dish from those lovely, capable hands. I'll do all the chopping, of course."

Images blossomed in her imagination. Of them sharing all the things they'd never shared before. Banter, relaxation and cheerful meal preparation, feeding each other bits and pieces, tasting their flavor and each other's reality and passion in playful kisses that would soon catch fire and turn desperate.

She thought she saw her own steaming, longing thoughts reflected in his eyes as they drained of mirth.

Suddenly he drawled, his voice nothing like the indulgent minute before, harsh, final, "I can make you stay."

Before outraged signals traveled from her brain to her hand to snatch his away, he removed it and added, "But I won't."

Her fingers curled on her plate's rim. "Wow, big of you. Just out of curiosity, how has that ego of yours told you that you have any control over my decisions and actions?"

He gave her a long considering look. "*Fácil.* You'll want another job with GAO in Brazil. Your *modus operandi* shows you're not interested in missions anywhere else. But if you leave, you won't get a job with GAO here again."

Fury spilled over, coursed through her like rivers of lava. "I'll prove to GAO that what you accused me of is untrue!"

He was all mock benign interest. "It is?"

She glowered at him for a full minute, rants and denials crashing in her head. Then suddenly a floodlight burst on in there. "Think about it, genius. If I were producing a reality show here, don't you think Qircamo's emergency would have been an explosive intro to the alleged pilot I'm supposedly putting together? Don't you think the film crew and my reality-show specialized director would have been the first people I had with me there? How do you explain that they weren't?"

"I would have stopped you. I would have kicked out any cameraman who tried to capitalize on an emergency I was handling, infringing my patient's privacy!"

"But you didn't need to, because I didn't call them. They signed a contract with me, setting the parameters of what they'd be allowed to film, and that they would film no one until we explained what we were doing and got full consent!"

"They signed a contract? With you? Not with GAO?"

"With me as GAO's representative. Before you came with your allegations, GAO was all for it. And, no, I'm not going to show it to you. You'd only scoff at a contract signed between 'partners in crime', wouldn't you?"

It was his turn to stare, that dark coppery tinge, which she'd only seen yesterday before he'd said he was sorry, and in the past during heights of arousal and moments of explosive release, imbuing his bronzed features.

At length, he dropped his gaze, exhaled. "Qircamo's emergency *was* premium drama. And the fact that you didn't capitalize on it—well, I told you I'm open to changing my mind. According to new evidence, I admit I may have been wrong."

"You *are* wrong. But you are here, and after this breakfast,

I am gone. I hope you can really handle this expedition and that you'll let the film crew stay and do what they've gone through a lot of effort and expense to do. You may not believe it but they are good people bent on delivering a service in their own field just as we are trying to do in ours. Or shall we say only *you* are, since according to you I'm here for contemptible reasons?"

He was silent for a long, long moment, his coppery color deepening. Then he raised his opal eyes. They now fired with every color there was and too many emotions to fathom.

Then he spoke and his voice, also fathomless, resonated its intensity in her every cell. "You make a watertight case for yourself. And I admit I built my conclusions about your intentions here on circumstantial evidence, interpreting every shred according to who you were in the past. Clearly, you're a different person now. So nothing I rationalized applies. As I said, I don't cling to my mistakes. I prefer the truth to my opinion of it, and it seems I owe you a big apology. I hope you'll accept it. And stay."

She felt as if she was drowning, almost wailed, *"I can't."*

His eyes suddenly narrowed, a ruthless gleam sparking in their depths. "I already told you that if you leave, you won't get another assignment with GAO. Not here."

"But—but you said…"

"I said I believe you, and I do. It has nothing to do with my earlier suspicions and it won't be GAO refusing you a new assignment. I want you to stay and I control eighty percent of GAO's operations in Brazil and have a big say in the remaining twenty percent."

She couldn't believe she was hearing this!

An indignant cry tore out of her. "This is coercion!"

His shrug was pragmatism incarnate. "Just a reality

check. But I said I won't force you to stay. You'll stay of your own volition."

"You think I'll stay after that?"

"You will if you're a professional. As you so adamantly told me yesterday, you're the one who masterminded this expedition. All the work you intended will still happen, the cause is still here and if you leave your team will suffer without their leader. All that's changed is that you have me and far more support and resources than you dreamed of. If you don't take this personally, you should be very glad I'm here."

"But you're *making* it personal!"

"It *is* personal. It doesn't get any more personal than marriage, *amor.*"

"We don't have a marriage, we have a marriage certificate. And you're not the epitome of professionalism if you let your desire to harass me endanger a mission of this importance."

His eyebrows rose in mock indignation. "I have no desire to harass you. I have every desire to devour you, though."

"And you still think we can work together like this?"

He leaned back, linked his hands behind his head, giving her a spectacular show of rippling muscles. "We did yesterday."

He did have a point. Yesterday had been a success by all professional measures. She even had to admit his technique had taught her a thing or two, too. And she *had* been looking forward to every minute of this expedition. So far it had turned out to be, while disturbing as hell, far more exciting and rewarding than anything she'd ever done before. Thanks to him.

Struggling for justifications to refuse to stay, her reasons dispersing with each moment, she opened her mouth with something that hadn't formed in her mind yet when he suddenly sat up in his chair, his head turned away, listening. Then she heard it, too. Calls. Merry ones this time.

"Ah, my team is here. The other part of your team now, *Jóia*." He jumped up to his feet, a knight's gallant gesture holding out his hand for hers. "Come meet them."

She shook her head. "You go ahead. I'll join you in a few minutes. I really need to fix myself a cup of tea. Want some?"

His fingers caressed her cheek. Then he bent and took her quivering lips in an exquisite kiss.

An endless moment later, he severed the connection, his lips reluctant. "Love some. Love all you've got to give." Before she dragged him down for a deeper plunge into that soul-shattering ritual, he straightened, prowled to the door, purring over his shoulder, "Don't be long."

She waited until he disappeared then let herself melt back on the chair like a deflated balloon.

If she had the least shred of survival instinct left, she'd up and run. What was going on? Why was he really doing this? Could he really want her genuinely now?

He hadn't wanted her in the past. He couldn't have. What had there been to want then? So their love-making had been real enough, but she believed that with his sex drive any hungry woman would have done, even the pathetic being she'd been.

But her plastic surgeon *had* worked magic. She'd seen the evidence of that in men's eyes and attentions. Maybe Roque with his fierce sexuality was reacting more powerfully to her reconstructed beauty? Yes, she could buy that.

But if so, what would his real desire do to her when his counterfeit one had almost wrecked her? And then he'd come here, thinking something so horrible of her—but no.

She couldn't use this as one of the reasons to deny him.

He'd already taken her word, admitted the new evidence of her actions so easily, had already apologized eloquently for suspecting her, admitted that she'd changed. Every word he'd said, every touch, every moment around him had felt so good, she'd forgotten anything could feel this way.

No—she shouldn't even think of succumbing to the temptation. She'd already used up all her breaks walking away from a hit-and-run and ending up whole and looking undamaged, no matter what she'd suffered to get this way. Life had offered her a mixture of indulgence and cruelty, but it was now offering her plain sailing and every opportunity to make a difference. She should cling to her new peace of mind.

Oh, who was she kidding? What peace of mind?

She may have functioned as if she'd forgotten Roque, but she hadn't.

She'd never defined the immense emotions she'd felt for him in the past, and only later had told herself those had been dependence, obsession, addiction, all spawned by her psychological upheaval at the time and all unhealthy and destructive.

She still didn't want to name those feelings. But one thing was unquestionable. What she'd felt *had* gone deep.

She'd be a fool to resurrect it.

CHAPTER SEVEN

"Ah, here she comes. Everyone, I want you to meet my wife and expedition co-leader, Dr. Jewel Johansson Da Costa."

The four people comprising Roque's team snapped around at his enthusiastic introduction. Their blast of interest almost stopped the sauntering Jewel in her tracks.

Next second he could see her modeling experience kicking in, her steps picking up speed, gaining that poised prowl of a woman used to people's admiration and way above caring about it one way or the other. She even turned carrying the mug of tea into a performance of grace.

Dawn was strengthening with the alarming speed it always did in the tropics, like someone pushing up the fader switch of a spotlight in a hurry. By the time she reached them he could see the three men now envied him, and the woman finally understood the reason behind his unattainability. But he still couldn't see Jewel's eyes well, couldn't read her reaction. And he realized something for the first time.

It had only been in her eyes, in her tone and body language that he'd been reading her reactions so far. Her face had lost some of its ability to display expression. That was an expected price of esthetic surgery. But he bet it was only noticeable to him, who'd made a habit of poring over her every nuance.

It frustrated him that he couldn't tell what her reaction was now to his proprietorial words, to his earlier ultimatum.

What was *he* thinking? Even when her face had had full expressiveness, he'd never really read her right. He'd only thought he had, until she'd proved him clueless.

Jewel stopped a couple of steps away, extended the mug to him with a smile that set his heart quivering and gave a general affable wave. Then she did something totally unexpected. She told him, and everyone else, exactly what she was thinking.

"Hi, everyone. I can see your surprise. Seems you didn't know Roque was married. You and me both! Till yesterday I had no idea Roque was still my husband. Now he says I'm also his co-leader, when yesterday he told me he has the leader spot all to his undisputed self and I'm to be his 'sidekick'. I *did* warn him about the dangers of me taking the term literally. Then just before you arrived he finished telling me it's either see this expedition through or find myself another country to work in, *then* proceeded to try to shame me into staying."

He guffawed at her brazen summary, at his team's stunned reaction to it. He took an eager step towards her. She didn't back away. "And did it work?"

She shrugged, looked at the others long-sufferingly. "Only because you might make a mess of things without me. I can't risk you messing up the expedition I've prepared for a year."

He laughed his immense relief and hugged her to his side.

The only woman on his team joined in the laughter, the first one to recover. "That's married talk all right. Delighted to meet you, Dr. Da Costa. Loretta Diaz, Roque's technical engineer."

Jewel shook her hand, grimacing, "Uh, let's keep Dr. Da Costa to Roque, OK? I'm either Jewel or JJ. Take your pick."

Another team member came forward to shake her hand. "Adalberto Alvarez, Roque's radiographer. Call me Berto or AA."

"AA makes you sound like a battery." Loretta snickered.

By the time introductions were over the sun was up and the pier was busy. Jewel led Roque's team around the boats and he followed a few steps away, succumbing to Berto's probing, his focus on Jewel. With every lively gesture, with every lilt of her animated tones, a skewer turned in his chest.

She'd never joked with him in the past. Outside the realm of physical intimacy where everything had been pure and sure, she'd felt so precarious he'd been so afraid to say anything that might have widened the gap he'd been struggling to obliterate. It had made him tense, unnatural, waiting for her to give him a sign she'd like a more spontaneous interaction between them. She hadn't, so there hadn't been any. Then she'd made sure there'd never be.

Now she was showing him how much fun she could be. Had this side of her never existed before? Or hadn't her uses for him extended to having fun this way…?

Stop it. It didn't matter any more. She had changed.

And though he did believe her, he couldn't be more thankful for the paranoid suspicions that had made him overcome his reluctance to see her again, made him come here braving resurrecting all the pain of the past, where he'd found this new Jewel. And they'd now share an incredible experience together, on every level. He'd make sure of that. What was more, she seemed to have accepted his presence, had shed her past pensiveness and the angst of the last day, and he couldn't wait to experience the full measure of her humor and spontaneity.

He got plenty of that as their teams were introduced. But

it wasn't directed solely at him, and by the time his team had installed his equipment in the two smaller boats comprising the convoy, he needed emergency one-on-one time with her.

She was having a laughing conversation with two of his men. On his approach they wandered off, giving him thumbs-ups and winks.

She turned to him, her open face radiant with an impish grin. "Is that what I should expect from now on? People dropping me in mid-sentence at your approach?"

He smiled, savoring the novel experience of being exposed to her acerbic wit. "Damned straight, as your people would say. They know better than to keep you occupied when I want you."

He waited for the indignation to come. It didn't. She only inclined her head at him. His heart teetered to the same angle in his chest. "It's not conductive to business to have everyone deserting me and leaving their posts whenever you get the urge."

He had to touch her, connect with her. He did, his hand reaching to her velvet cheek. "You're probably right. As that urge is perpetual."

Her eyes dimmed. He almost snatched his hand away, made an encompassing gesture with it. He had to restore her smile! "What's your opinion of my team? My facilities? Now you can really call the expedition multi-disciplinary, eh?"

His tension eased a bit when her eyes warmed. "Your people are great. I've never met anyone in this line of business who wasn't. As for your facilities, you're suffering from a condition called 'I know my stuff inside and out I think everyone must too'."

His laugh boomed at her teasing, his heart too, with relief. Now he'd experienced ease with her, he never wanted to go back to friction. "I didn't know it was a condition."

"It is, and very hard to treat, too. Not terminal but terminally aggravating to the people interacting with the sufferer."

"Is treatment forcing the sufferer to explain his 'stuff'?"

She gave a sage nod. "The only known treatment."

Smiling broadly, he bowed and swept an arm out in invitation. "Lead the way to the treatment room."

She chuckled and preceded him. He followed a step behind her, to watch her move.

He couldn't wait to have her alone, made an imperative gesture that made his guards jump to the pier at once. He went ahead of her now, tugging her by the hand inside, hurrying her up. Sudden cries ripped through the air, through both of them.

They swung around, found Madeline running with a boy of no more than two in her arms, with Inácio and four locals, two women and two older children, running in her wake.

His aroused agitation turned off abruptly, his surgeon side coming to the fore as he rushed to meet the emergency, feeling Jewel keeping up with him step for step.

He took the little boy from Madeline as she panted, "We only understood that he fell! He has a huge scalp hematoma."

Roque felt the bulge in the toddler's head that had formed her impromptu diagnosis. He didn't think it was that simple.

"Get Loretta and Berto," he barked, and turned to rush inside the boat. Someone clung to him, stopped his dash. He turned his eyes way down, met the streaming eyes of a woman who was shaking and babbling, her fingers digging into his arm. Sympathy shot through him with her tremors, hot and deep. She had to be the boy's mother.

She was. He struggled to understand her torrent as his clinical senses went into hyperdrive, taking in everything about the little boy, documenting, cross-referencing, concluding.

Then he felt Jewel's soft hands on his arm. "Give me the boy, Roque. You get some history and I'll do emergency measures."

He relinquished the boy to her and she received him with great gentleness, her face full of compassion. Roque walked behind her in a trance, a part of him listening to the mother's agitated account, all others buried under an avalanche of pain.

The child he and Jewel had lost would have been seven now. And there could have been others. Even one this boy's age. He'd wanted to fill his world with replicas of her to love and cherish.

His first and only brush with happiness had been when she'd become pregnant with his baby; his first tumble into despair had been when she'd lost it. But he'd held himself together, soothed her, told her there'd be other babies. And she'd only said, "Never."

He'd tried to remain calm, sworn he understood her trauma, would only ask they try again when she was ready, but he *had* to have children. One at least.

It had been then that she'd told him that her pregnancy had been a mistake when maintenance drugs had deactivated the Pill. Then she'd told him why she'd married him.

He now watched her placing the boy on the examination table as if he was precious to her. Why hadn't his child been?

The mother's agitation encroached on his, dragged his focus back to her. He soothed her as he asked her baby's name, asked her more questions. He joined Jewel only when she'd finished assessing the child, when he had himself under control.

"His name is Ake," he said as he performed a full neurological exam of the boy, avoiding looking at his face or making eye contact with her. He felt her give a sad nod, knew where her eyes touched him, where his face burned.

"It's a growing skull fracture, isn't it?" she whispered.

His eyes made an unwilling swing to hers. She'd diagnosed it, and that easily? As a rare complication of skull fractures, it should have been one of the last things she'd thought of. The progressive enlargement of the fracture line led to protrusion of the skull contents with the fast growth rate of the brain at that age. But as it was also known as a leptomeningeal cyst because it was usually associated with a cystic mass filled with cerebrospinal fluid—what Madeline had mistaken for a hematoma—it was very hard to diagnose. But Jewel hadn't been fooled.

He didn't want to feel impressed. Not right now.

He gave her his reluctant corroboration. "Yes. Little Ake here fell on his head three months ago. He screamed and fussed then it passed. A month ago this bulge began to form over his left parietal region, but as he made no complaints, they didn't worry. But the rate of enlargement increased and he began to be lethargic and disoriented, and today he just didn't wake up."

"As horrible as this is," she murmured, her voice a difficult rasp, "Ake is still lucky—that you're here, and that his general condition and neurological status are stable enough so you can operate…" Urgency permeated her gaze. He almost looked away from the lacerating emotion. "You will, won't you?"

The idea of operating on a child constricted his heart. He steered clear of pediatric cases if he could. He couldn't now. His nod was slow, unwilling. "As soon as I obtain scans."

She snapped a fraught look at the tiny inert Ake then turned hopeful eyes to Roque. "Can I assist?"

His heart convulsed this time. Before he could answer, rushing footsteps had both of them turning to the incomers. Loretta, Berto and Madeline. The first two rushed to the PET-CT scanner. Madeline joined him and Jewel.

"Inácio and the others are keeping the peace outside with the guards," Madeline gasped. "A very distraught father and what looks like the whole tribe seem to be all accounted for now."

Roque only nodded to her, thankful for her interruption, and turned to prepare Ake for the scan. Jewel followed his instructions, extracted the radioactive tracer glucose from his supplies, injected the boy as Madeline winced and moaned over the far worse diagnosis they'd reached.

Loretta and Berto operated the scanner, sent its sliding table gliding out, then Berto called out, "All set, Roque."

Roque scooped up the child, gently put him in place. "Give me a skull series. Let's look at the neck, too."

"Is this a CT scanner? I've never seen one that small!" Madeline exclaimed.

It was Jewel who answered her. "That's a PET-CT scanner, Maddy. I'm not surprised you've never seen one—they're so expensive most hospitals don't have it."

Madeline frowned. "Um, PET is positron emission tomography?"

Jewel didn't answer right away, her eyes clinging to Ake as his flimsy body slid inside the machine. Roque didn't feel like talking at all. He wasn't in an educational mood.

At length Jewel looked up at her nurse. "Yes. But this combined scanner gives comprehensive and in-depth scans of injuries and their pathological effects. The CT component shows anatomical defects and the PET one shows deranged tissue metabolism. In the PET scan inflamed tissues show up as brightly colored areas."

Jewel's eyes turned to Roque, asking if he had anything to add. A respectful bow of his head conceded she was doing a good job. His "impressed" factor was rising by the minute.

She seemed to be well versed in the latest technology. Seemed his contribution was the only area where she was ignorant.

Madeline's question interrupted his oppressive thoughts. "Joo said you made some huge innovations. Is this one of them?"

Suddenly an alien feeling took him over. The need to brag. *Deus,* he was having the primitive urge to chest-thump for his woman. There went all his illusions of being an advanced being.

Thankfully it was Loretta who answered for him, saving him from sounding like a self-satisfied fool. "He may not have invented it but he made it smaller, faster and more effective. This darling he modified goes through scans at hyper-speed— 64 slices per second was a dream until he made it a reality."

Silence followed Loretta's answer as they prepared the surgical station and themselves. All through it he kept snatching looks at Jewel. It stunned him to find his heart ramming his ribcage, still waiting for her reaction to Loretta's information. But it wasn't Jewel who eventually reacted. It was Madeline who deluged him in admiration and interest.

In minutes Loretta displayed the scans on the computer screen. As he and Jewel converged to view them, Roque shook off his dejection, focused on his chore.

"This looks bad," Jewel choked.

It did. It was.

He took a deep inhalation. "OK, to business. First, to maintain intracranial pressure during the procedure."

"Mannitol now and keeping up oxygen pressure during the surgery?" Jewel sought his approval.

Her knowledge shouldn't surprise him any more. She seemed to be a comprehensive field doctor. He nodded and began anesthesia.

After Jewel had finished her task she took his assistant's

position and he made the first incision into the scalp, a horse-shoe-shaped cut over the bony protrusion.

Step by step, he and Jewel worked quickly to repair the tears in the damaged tissue and cauterized bleeding arteries. Roque handed bony fragments to Madeline to soak in an anti-biotic solution before he wired larger pieces together.

With Madeline informing them that the child's condition was deteriorating, he and Jewel rushed through the reconstruction of the skull, then scalp closure.

After they finished post-operative details, Jewel's old pensive air hung around her like a cloak, making him almost throw the others out so he could grab her, question her. Why was it back? Was she, too, thinking of their lost child…?

But he still needed his other colleagues around as he detailed Ake's continuing care. Then he had to organize a helicopter to transfer Ake to his hospital as soon as he cleared Recovery for the intensive care he'd need and to prepare his parents' accommodations for the months of rehabilitation ahead.

He gritted his teeth, took care of business, resigned that it would be a while until he was alone again with Jewel.

CHAPTER EIGHT

JEWEL made sure she wasn't alone with Roque again.

After the surgery had ended, he'd almost snared her into another tête-à-tête at one point, but she'd been saved when his team had roped him in to handle the last-minute details of Ake's transfer. She'd walked away, shaking with the reprieve, praying for something that would assure her of more time away from him.

Then she'd gotten it. A chance to get away for hours.

Qircamo had regained consciousness and had asked for the people who'd healed him. His people had come hastening to fetch them. And she'd grabbed Inácio, two guards and Montoya, their expert on the indigenous people, and gone with the tribesmen.

Not only was she certain she could do the follow-up on Qircamo on her own, she needed the long, bumpy drive to assimilate her turmoil. To thwart her, her four companions were in a talkative mood. She could ask them to shut up or she could participate. She participated.

And here they were, at their destination, and her chaotic thoughts were engulfed in the press of people, the demands of work and the wonder of meeting her first real-life shaman.

Qircamo, now that he was conscious, had a permeating presence that made her very self-conscious of everything she did under his scrutiny. Her hands shook as she removed his bandages and packs, her mind streaking ahead with worst-case scenarios. Then she saw his leg and all her tension evaporated. She raised relieved eyes from her examination to meet a gaze that was fathomless with ancient knowledge and infinite patience and benevolence.

"Qircamo—if I may call you that—you must really have powerful magic," she whispered to the old man in Portuguese. His weathered face crinkled with understanding, on every level. She smiled back at him, thankful for his improvement and that she'd had any role in it. "Your general condition is excellent. As for your leg, you'll be walking the forest for years to come."

"It's you and your man who had the magic," he said in heavily accented Portuguese, his bony hand patting her hand. She fisted it around a stab of pain the moment he'd said "your man." "I thank both of you for my life—and my leg. I'll pray to the gods to bless you."

She swallowed, shook her head. "It's my—my partner they should bless. He was the one who saved your leg."

He looked at her for a long moment. Then his incredible face creased in what had to be ultimate serenity. "I believe you are all the blessing he wants from the gods."

"Oh…" His words struck her hard for being so wrong, with the brutal, idiotic wish that they weren't.

She thanked God for the distraction of having a lot to do before this was over. She busied herself with getting rid of his bloodied packs, applying fresh ones, upping his antibiotics, all the time feeling his penetrating gaze probing her.

Then, with Montoya translating the more involved words,

she advised Qircamo and his people about his continued care and said she'd be back in forty-eight hours to close his wounds.

As Inácio gathered their things, she succumbed to an impulse, and bent and kissed Qircamo's leathery cheek.

"Obrigado," she whispered.

As she rushed out of his tent, she didn't know what she'd thanked him for. For bringing her and Roque together for real for the first time? For planting that damaging hope that he did have clairvoyance and could see what lay in Roque's heart? Or was she just delirious with lack of sleep?

The tribe insisted on offering her festive food and drink in gratitude again, and it was over two more hours before they finally started on their way back to the pier.

Once in the truck, Jewel sank back into her turbulent thoughts. This time her companions left her alone.

She still couldn't get over it, seeing Roque with Ake, the infinite empathy and gentleness that had permeated his every glance and move. It had hurt. Was still hurting.

Would he have been like this with their own child, had he or she lived? She'd never let herself think what it would have been like, had chosen to believe his jubilation over her pregnancy, his despair over her miscarriage had been part and parcel of him wanting to cement their marriage for his own ends. She'd always been ready to believe any ulterior motive to explain his behavior.

In the past, that had been somewhat justified. But now she couldn't cling to the anesthetizing misconceptions. He didn't have a petty or exploitative bone in his body. She doubted he'd ever had any, no matter what his situation had been then. Now, even in his current superior position, she believed he hadn't meant his threat of depriving her of assignments with GAO, that he had just been emphasizing how much he wanted her to stay. How much he wanted her, period. And in her restored physical condition, she no longer found it hard to believe he could want her for herself.

And though she knew his desire could be nowhere as sublime as Qircamo had painted it, that it was only physical, that had been all she'd ever wished for. His honest desire. And now she saw who he was, or who he'd become, she felt no shame in wanting it. In wanting him. She felt only breathless anticipation.

If he was offering his honest desire now, no matter what happened later, she was taking all she could of it. And him.

He couldn't find Jewel.

It had been five hours and thirteen minutes since he'd last seen her. Over the endless, agonizing hours, his fear that she might have changed her mind again and had left after all had metamorphosed into a far worse dread.

What if someone had abducted her under his very nose?

Too agitated to take inventory of who else might be missing, he'd looked everywhere, questioned everyone, until a local had saved him from an impending heart attack just minutes ago. He'd seen Jewel leaving with some men from her team.

She hadn't been abducted! *Agradeça O Deus.*

But this could still mean she *had* left. She could have had some of her team transport her to Tabatinga's airport.

Not if he had anything to say about it. Even if she had left Tabatinga, left Brazil, he'd go after her, drag her back. She wasn't walking out on him again…

Stop. Think. He did, took half a dozen steadying inhalations. He'd been by her cabin four times. He'd check again. This time he'd enter it, make sure she was still here.

As he tore his way there, people jumped out of his path as

if from that of a speeding car. In under two minutes he reached the cabin, reached for the doorknob—and it receded out of reach.

His heart surged in relief. *Jewel. She's back. She's here.*

Next moment it did so again, in dismay. *Not Jewel, not Jewel.* The frustrated mantra churned in his head.

It was Madeline. And she let out a startled shriek. "*Dr. Da Costa*—Roque—you just knocked ten years off my life expectancy!"

"What are you doing here? Where's Jewel?" he growled.

"Er…I'm staying here. I share the cabin with Jewel, and I haven't seen her in a while. She'll probably come back any moment now for her afternoon shower. The indoor one, that is."

"Her things are still here? She hasn't left?"

"Uh, I haven't looked, but—"

He pushed past the woman, no longer seeing or hearing her.

Jewel. That was all that boomed in his head and chest. He had to see for himself if she was still here. This woman could be stalling him until Jewel got far enough away.

The dresser had combs and hair products on it. He knew Jewel didn't use any. She just washed her hair, ran her fingers through it and left it to dry into that glorious cascade.

There were two small suitcases. He couldn't tell if either was the one he'd seen Jewel packing. Both could be Madeline's. Only finding Jewel's clothes would be proof. The closet.

He snatched it open, found six outfits hanging there, utilitarian, similar-colored, their loose-fitting size not indicative of whom they belonged to. How could he tell if any were hers? If Madeline was covering for her, she wasn't about to tell him which was which. There was only one way to find out.

He took each out, sniffed it. The first one wasn't Jewel's. Or the second. Or the third. The fourth brought her scent, hitting him in the solar plexus, in the loins. Jewel. She was still here. Or had she left one outfit behind to throw him off?

Deus, what was happening to him? He was behaving like a lunatic. A dangerously paranoid lunatic to boot.

"So this is the kind of supervision I have to expect on this expedition, huh?" Jewel's voice poured all over him, cool, smirking, and, *Deus*, so welcome.

He swung around to her, images cascading in his mind. Shooing Madeline out of the room, locking the door behind her and dragging Jewel into his arms, crushing her there to make sure she was really here, then dragging her to bed and drowning in her. The pressure of the urges made him light-headed.

Jewel's velvet drawl worsened his condition. "You're going to be inspecting my clothes for signs of lack of deodorant use?"

"Where have you been?" *Sim,* very good indeed. Now he sounded like an insecure, jealous fool. One with a fetish for sniffing his woman's clothes. *Get a hold of yourself,* idiota.

"Why? I'm supposed to report my movements to you?"

"*Sim,* you damn well are. Do you realize just how dangerous this place is for a woman like you?"

Her exquisite, dense eyebrows shot up. "A woman like me? I'm a sort now? Or do you mean just any woman?"

"No! I mean *you!* A woman any male would go to any lengths to sink his teeth into!"

Her lips twitched. "I don't see any male baring his fangs at me. Of course, if you're talking about your own fantasies…"

He advanced on her, vibrating to the frequency of every urgent emotion there was. "Never fear, I'm going to demonstrate every one of those in detail. But you're not sidetracking me. You are *not* to make one move without company and protection!"

The eyebrow that arched at him now was in itself a portrait of mischief. "I had both, but thank you so much for caring."

"I don't care who you had with you. You don't move around without *my* company and protection. Is that understood?"

"I had four men along, two of them armed to the teeth. You consider yourself better than that?"

"Damn right, I am. Get this straight, Jewel—"

"Uh, *guys*." Madeline raised her voice from the door. "I'll go get a bite to eat. Try not to burn the place down, OK?" With that she turned and escaped the scene.

Jewel gazed after her for a second then stuck her fists at her waist. "What's that? Payback for embarrassing you in front of your team? You've got only yourself to blame for that."

"Did I look embarrassed to you? Trust me when I say I'm embarrassment-proof. This is for making me think…"

He stopped. He had to stop. He was taking this beyond foolishness. She was here. She was safe. And she was staying. That was all that mattered. He shouldn't take his agitation out on her.

She cocked her lovely head at him. "What did you think? That I'd left? That I skulked behind your back instead of confronting you? As you said, I wouldn't do that to my team. And since when have I left without telling you what I intended?"

It was as if something detonated inside his head.

He looked down on her for a whole minute, grappling with the blast of fury and revisited humiliation and pain.

He finally snarled, "If you mean you walking out on me, let me refresh your memory. You didn't tell me your intention of leaving me, I cornered you into it. I offered to take you back to the States to recuperate among familiar scenes and people after—after your miscarriage, and you jumped at the offer, no doubt thinking it the best way to go and never come back without a confrontation. I'm sure if I hadn't given you that opening you *would* have skulked behind my back. But fool that I was, I messed up your plans, didn't I? I insisted on taking you back myself, left you no choice but to tell me exactly why you'd married me so I'd back down. You even asked me my price for all the times I'd performed in bed with you. Say, I never asked—how much *did* you intend to pay me per session? At what price did you rate me?"

His question rang in the suddenly crushing silence. Her face went totally still, even her eyes stopped transmitting any expression. Dammit, what was she thinking?

Again she did the unexpected. She looked him straight in the eyes and told him exactly what she was thinking.

"Would it satisfy you if I told you I thought a fair settlement was everything I had and would ever have?"

The import of her words, the sincerity permeating them—it was too much for him to handle, too great to contain. He had to—had to…

He growled incoherently and snatched at her. She completed the yank that brought her slamming into his body with a surge of her own, met his crushing kiss halfway.

He sank into her, lips and tongue and teeth, devouring her gasps in a savage mouth that would have forced hers open had it not already done so, hungrily. His teeth sank into her lips, his tongue plunging deep inside her, driving in furious rhythms, draining her, growling for more. She gave him more, opened for him, let him ravage her, take his fill, then plunge even deeper. He pushed her onto the bed and this time, when she staggered back, she dragged him down with her on purpose, her hands convulsing on his bunched muscles, revealing their need for his feel, his closeness, his impact.

He gave them all to her, coming down on top of her, taking enough of his weight off so he wouldn't hurt her, giving her enough to assuage her clamoring, and his.

The moment he filled her arms, her head flung back, sending

her hair fanning out in a shimmering fan, and something unintelligible tore out of her lungs. It sounded like "so good."

It *was,* magnificent beyond description. Their eyes and breaths tangling, their hands roaming each other in disbelieving wonder, her feel cushioning him, her voluptuousness reveling in his toughness, her legs winding tight around his hips, then higher on his back, in ultimate invitation. He tossed his head back and growled something as fierce.

Then it shot to a higher level. He didn't know when the initial ferocity metamorphosed into something far more overpowering, something as profound and penetrating as it was tender and tempestuous. He enveloped himself in her arms, her kiss, her eagerness, one thing reverberating in his mind.

This was new.

He remembered how her younger body and passion had felt colliding with his, merging, feeding, sending his conflagration higher. And this was nothing like it. She'd never driven him beyond that last barrier of control like now, had never sent his mind unraveling, his senses stampeding. Never, not even with her, had he bypassed the build-up of arousal to the fever pitch of mindlessness in heartbeats like this.

In mortification, he realized that one thing was the same. *He* was. Repeating his mistakes.

He'd always rushed her, pursued her, besieged her, afraid to let her blood cool, her logic return, making him lose any chance with her. And where had that method gotten him?

A day ago she'd been hating him, shocked to find them still legally tied. Then the moment she relented, responded, he was dragging her into ultimate intimacies that were bound to muddy everything. Again he was giving her no chance to make a reasoned decision she could defend to herself once satisfaction faded and her body stopped crying out for his. Once again he was placing himself in a position where he only represented sex to her.

No wonder she'd treated him like she would have a gigolo. In the past, when he'd felt he hadn't been reaching her on an emotional level, he *had* used sex to capture her, to try to keep her.

But he wasn't doing it again! He had to have her wanting all of him, not only what he could make her feel. This time she wouldn't have him that easily. Easy come, easy to let go.

But she was writhing beneath him, her passion igniting his higher, her lips moaning her hunger and pleasure under his, her hands worshipping him all over, kneading, needing. *Now.*

His lips and hands worshipped her back, the power of a bursting dam, eight years' worth of pent-up craving and bitterness behind every shaking breath and touch and grasp.

He couldn't do it. Couldn't deny her…

No—he had to! If he was to ever mean more than sex to her…

But her need and surrender were tearing at his self-control. He shuddered, couldn't stop giving in to her, giving her, stroking and kneading and pleasuring her.

Just one more taste—please, everything in him begged.

Helpless, lost, conceding her power and his defeat, he plunged into their fusion again, his lips gliding his restless hunger along her velvet sweetness, absorbing all he could of her heat and moans, hoarding her feel and eagerness.

Feeling her craving him, needing him was all he'd ever wanted from this life. It tampered with his will and sanity all over again. But it was a matter of survival this time that he made sure her desire transcended the physical. He had to take drastic measures—now.

He came up from their last and deepest merging panting, broke out of her feverish embrace.

He almost fell back into her trembling arms when her sob of "Roque, please…" speared through him.

He crushed down on the overriding temptation instead, lifted himself away on shaking arms. Her legs unlocked with his move, fell to his sides, rubbing, urging. He gritted his teeth.

"*Sim, Jóia.* I will please you—please you until you fall apart with pleasure, then I'll please you again until you're mad, until you're finished…" He dimly wondered if his potency would survive the blow. Then he delivered it. "But not now."

CHAPTER NINE

"TELL ME we're really going to do it now!"

Jewel bit back a snappy answer, pointed at the boat that was moving away from the pier, what they now called "Roque's Boat." "Where our fearless leader goes, we follow, Maddy."

To underline the accuracy of her words, their own river-boat gave a long bass honk and in minutes they were following the two smaller boats, finally starting the trek to one of the least explored tributaries of the Amazon River and one of the last wild places on earth.

They should have left three days ago. But Roque had decreed that they would wait that much longer to close Qircamo's wounds. It had been five days since Roque had come back into her life.

And they'd been five days of the weirdest kind of hell.

Roque was driving her insane. He'd already driven her past inhibitions, confusion and suspicions. Not to mention bitterness, insecurities and long-held prejudices. And it had taken him a whopping twenty-four hours to do it. Then, just as he'd had her total surrender, he'd walked away.

The whisper that had gashed her when he'd extricated

himself from her arms, ignoring her pleas for him to take her now, now, echoed in her mind again.

"Secure in your one-hundred-percent results again? Got me to admit how much I want you, so you'd be the one to walk away this time?" she'd demanded.

He'd walked back to her then, knelt on the deck beside her, his eyes predatory, sending the unabated hunger inside her howling. "That's the biggest load of rubbish I've ever heard. I'm walking away from you probably at the cost of my potency." He'd pressed her hand to his rock-hardness for proof. "But I'm done doing things backwards. Satisfaction before anticipation, intimacy before courtship." Then he'd exploded out of the cabin.

And it made no sense! He *should* be seeking retribution. Her past insults, now it seemed they'd been undeserved, had been unforgivable. Men held undying grudges for far less.

Yet he behaved as if he wasn't holding any. So what did it mean when a man held back from slaking his lust? When he talked of anticipation and courtship? Could that mean he wanted to make their stunted marriage into something more? Why? Did she?

No! She didn't. She—she… It didn't *matter* what she wanted!

But she wanted to be with him, for as long as his new desire lasted, and had told him that, in words and actions. And he wouldn't let her!

Inside, she floundered. Outside, she took him on in duels of wit she'd come to crave. It was glorious talking to him, doing things with him—just being with him. They'd never talked or shared before. That had been her mistake. She'd been such a mess back then.

But she was healed now. In body and mind and mood. And Roque made her head spin and heart soar with what he was.

Effortless leader, gifted doctor, loyalty-inspiring friend, gallant gentleman, thrilling companion. And to make it worse, he kept switching from blasé seducer to single-minded devourer.

Just thinking of him made her heart storm and her body burn. She fidgeted as Tabatinga receded and nature took over. The boats sailed nearer one bank, offering them heart-soaring views of incredible forests, wading birds and fresh-water pink dolphins. The for-once-struck-silent Madeline was snapping away with her digital camera.

At last Madeline's enthusiasm bubbled over. "Yippee! My first Amazonian experience! At last! Man, I can't wait to go on those aluminum boat side-stream trips. Monkeys, parrots, butterflies, orchids…ah! And the night trips Roque promised! Owls, caimans, and those weird birds—those potoos he mentioned…"

"Don't forget the jaguars, alligators, boa constrictors and anacondas!" Jewel added in mock malice, Madeline's oblivious cheerfulness grating a bit in her raw condition.

Momentary alarm flitted in Madeline's eyes before she wrinkled her nose. "Oh, hush. I'm in raptures of expectation now—of the hikes to see the giant forests and the riverside communities, of bartering for some honest-to-goodness indigenous handcrafts and getting a bona fide Amazonian tribal tattoo!"

Jewel cast a wide glance out into the seemingly bankless river as their riverboat followed the smaller boats' lead midstream and sighed. "Glad you're so happy, Maddy."

"Who wouldn't be? I'm on the *Amazon River.* Tell me all you know about it, Joo. I bet you know everything!"

Jewel sighed again. "No one knows everything about anything, Maddy, least of all Amazonia. The forest keeps most of its secrets. It isn't hard as it covers half of Brazil and extends into six other countries. But, yes, your beloved Amazon River *is* longer than the Nile."

Madeline gaped. "How did you know I was going to ask that?"

Jewel crooked her a complacent smile. "So-called modern people are pathetically predictable."

She submitted to Madeline's equally predictable shove as she tried to keep her eyes off Roque's boat now that he'd come on the observation deck.

He stood there like a conqueror of old, power and distinction stamped in his every line. And control. Talk about control. Then he waved.

Madeline waved back enthusiastically. It figured. Jewel bet females of all species in a hundred miles' radius were waving right back at him. She wouldn't be one of them, just this once.

At her ignoring him, he cocked his head, tension gathering in his stance. Then he pressed his fingers to his lips for a drawn-out moment. Her heart pounded at the pantomime. She knew his fingers were a substitute for her lips, for every other part of her he'd told her he was dying to taste, to pleasure. Her nerves fired when he released the kiss, let it blow her way. She almost growled at her pathetic reaction.

Next second he swung around and rushed out of sight, seemingly in answer to some summons.

"So..." Madeline resumed with ultra-brightness. "The brochure said among the estimated 15,000 species here, thousands aren't classified. How did they count them if they're not classified?"

Jewel sighed. "Counted is one thing, classified is another. If you must know the difference I'll hand you over to our naturalist. He's dying for an excuse to drown in your sapphire eyes."

"What?" Madeline yelped in elated surprise. "Marcos? That dimpled hunk dripping in Indiana Jones appeal? No way!"

"Yes way. That's what you miss when you focus all your attention in the wrong direction, Maddy."

"Meaning in yours and Roque's? Can you blame me? I'm still stunned you're married, and to a world-leading genius who's a world-class hunk. Your family sure never went public with that piece of explosive news."

"They didn't because at the time Roque was a doctor who survived on grants and had a one-room condo in Rio and no car. It was the far lesser evil to advertise that I'd gone mad and went to live in the jungle than make my marriage to him public."

"I bet your folks would love to call him son-in-law now."

Jewel sighed in bitterness. "Yeah, I bet."

"But cut your folks some slack, who wouldn't? That man of yours is something else."

Jewel almost stamped her foot. He wasn't her man. She had no idea what he was, or what he wanted to be.

Madeline went on, "But you guys seem to have such a complicated history, I doubt either of you understands it."

Jewel exhaled another dejected sigh. "It was too naïve to think you'd resist the urge to gossip, wasn't it, Maddy?"

"It's not gossip as it's staying between us!" Madeline scrunched up her eyes against the sun, indignant. "You're my friend and I'm concerned. And I'm confused. But I bet not half as much as both of you are."

"I don't know why you include Roque in your summation. He certainly isn't confused about anything."

"You're just spinning so hard you can't see him spinning. Seriously, Joo, yours is a match made in a higher echelon of heaven. Two magnificent creatures who burn the air in a mile radius around them and who also share the same vocation."

"I didn't share Roque's vocation when he married me. The truth is, I have no clue why he did marry me."

"Because he loved—loves—you, why else?"

Jewel chewed her lip, feeling her confusion only mounting. This couldn't have been why he'd married her. But she no longer had theories why he had.

Madeline went on, "And he's here seeking you again, and you've both changed, for the best, so what's stopping you from coming back together?"

Jewel sighed. "Would you believe—him?"

Madeline's mouth clunked open. "Huh?"

"Threw a sabot in the cogs of your logic machine, huh?"

"Hey, give me a break. I thought you were the one resisting the reunion, but if he's the one who's—aargh! I give up!"

Jewel's gaze swept the endless expanse of glasslike waters, let its serenity permeate her, let Madeline's last three words seep their resignation through her.

Then she finally said, "Yeah. Me, too."

"Are you coming, too, or shall I go alone?"

Roque watched Jewel's flushed lips caressing the words, heard her rich tones undulating to their rhythm. But he couldn't understand a thing.

"Earth to Roque! You can come down from orbit now."

Her smile was a shard of light and delight piercing his heart. He rose under her influence, his hand sweeping a hungry path from a strong calf, exposed by knee-long shorts, up to her waist. "Can't I remain lost in orbit, mapping your topography?"

Half a giggling pirouette took her out of reach. "You don't seem so lost now. And now you've landed safely, are you coming? I can go alone if you'd rather stay here."

"You've such a short memory. I said you go nowhere without me."

She wrinkled her nose at him. "You said that ages ago."

"Thirteen days and…" he consulted his watch "…fourteen hours and twenty-three, *four* minutes ago."

She gave him a mysterious look, her eyes going a murky shade of honey. Then her lips parted, the smile vacant this time. "Come on, then. I'd rather avoid another macho attack."

With this she spun around, called to the team she'd chosen for their landing and first visit to one of their targeted tribes.

He followed, his steps slower, his heart racing.

Just what had he thought? That her surrender had been a *carte blanche* and he was free to pick it up whenever he pleased?

Well, surprise. Seemed she'd withdrawn it. Maybe had torn it up and burned it, too. And he had only himself to blame.

Her withdrawal had started the day they'd embarked on their journey, in subtle ways. Giving him no chance to find her alone, emptying her words and glances of familiarity until she interacted with him with the same neutral ease and distance she did with the rest of the men on the expedition. He hadn't noticed right away, lost in discovering the new her, all that appealed to his every fastidious taste and satisfied his every uncompromising demand, and struggling to remember why he'd started this, and what was so bad about her craving him, too.

The sobering answer always reared its head. She'd craved him once before, and he'd splurged himself on her and she'd ended up reviling him, sated and sickened.

But he'd almost reached a point where even this argument couldn't dam the hunger, where everything inside him clamored to have her now, come what may. But he couldn't, had to wait. And, then, she seemed no longer interested anyway…

"May we ask a question and not be thrown overboard?"

Roque blinked. Berto. And Loretta. And they were standing right in front of him. Where had they come from?

"You'll be thrown overboard if you don't make it quick!" he barked, his annoyance taking a short cut to maximum.

The duo exchanged a wary glance, seemed to agree that Berto should deliver the question. "Joo's team know who's doing what. *We're* sort of lost until *our* boss decides our fate."

"Call her Joo one more time, Berto, and you'd better learn to swim in a hurry."

Inferno. His condition was more critical than he'd realized. Not only did he sound like a jealous adolescent, he was acting like one. And slipping in his leader role, too.

Had she left his team floundering on purpose to point this out? Or was she keeping out of his territory to avoid another "macho attack" as she'd put it? Or what had come after it…?

This was getting ridiculous, these attacks of absent-mindedness. He gritted his teeth. "You two, come with me."

In ten minutes they were all aboard two rowing boats. He took over rowing his boat, the grueling exercise and the 110°F temperature easing his agitation.

He didn't see the wild beauty they were nearing. He was in a limbo of blurred images and sensations, with only Jewel in focus. Her closeness and connection had been his first taste of true living. And now she was drifting away again, and he couldn't…

"But if it's better for indigenous people to be left uncontacted by Western civilization, why are we going there?" Madeline's question intruded into his oppression. Thankfully.

Jewel answered, sitting further away from him than Madeline, yet her voice felt closer, almost inside his head.

"We'll try to undo the damage done by past contacts, Maddy. Even those with the best intentions resulted in disaster when the tribes were exposed to Western infectious diseases, the ones you and I take in our stride but to which they have no immunity."

Madeline persisted. "Then why go after those who haven't been contacted at all? Won't *we* bring them our antibiotic-resistant strains and vaccination-fortified viruses?"

Jewel sighed. "Contacting unknown tribes will remain controversial. But beside the dangers of imported infections, they have other endemic health problems that can't be handled by traditional remedies. And those specific people we're visiting *have* been discovered. It's better that we make first contact than anyone else."

Perpetually simmering fury and futility made Roque interrupt. "You didn't mention what really drives these people to extinction, Jewel. Once the modern world intrudes, those people fragment and disperse. Then they're no more. Or, worse, they become like Qircamo's tribe, both cut off from tradition and incapable of joining the modern world."

"Protecting indigenous people from the outside world *has* become an important goal of the Brazilian government and its Federal Department, Roque," Berto put in.

Roque gave the oar an extra-hard yank, jerking the whole boat. "So Vale do Javari has been declared an indigenous reservation, but did that stop the cattle, logging and mining interests from continuing their pressures? What really galls me is that the uncontacted tribes are remnants of former indigenous nations who fled deeper into the jungle after violent encounters with the outside world. Yet no matter how far they run or how deep they hide, it keeps encroaching, leaving them no escape."

Silence met his frustrated rage. It lasted until they went

ashore and started to trek into the forest. He fell in step with Jewel, and Madeline strode ahead, leaving them alone.

Jewel's eyes briefly swept to him before snapping back to negotiate the thickening undergrowth covering the forest bed. He wanted to stop her, take her in his arms, rest her head over his heart, let the contact soothe him, defuse him. He hadn't had anything of her in days and he was suffering.

She suddenly talked. "The indigenous people situation *is* frustrating as hell. And I know that whatever we do may seem useless, ultimately. Yet we have to try and help them in any way we can, and hope. But no matter how committed I am to this, I guess you're bound to feel more so, may even feel in a way responsible as it's your people who're driving those people to extinction."

Her words fell on him like a wrecking ball. It took him a full minute before he was able to articulate an answer.

Then he rasped it. "You think I'm of Portugese origins? Another assumption, eh? But what's another one in the sea of careless conjectures that form my character in your mind?"

He hadn't meant it to come out so cold and mocking. So hurt. But it had and he couldn't recall it, was in no mental shape to apply any brakes. Her golden eyes poured startled confusion over him and his control fractured.

So she'd lost interest already, eh? Even before she had him this time? *Bom,* let him give her one more good reason—the *best* reason possible—to thank God for her lucky escape, to congratulate herself for gauging his worth correctly and discarding him like the trash that she thought he was.

"Are you going by my physical appearance in your assumption?" he rasped an abrasive sneer. "Or is it my family names? I'm sure there are existing families with those names, but in my case they're just a random combination my illegitimate orphan mother picked from the obituaries right before she had me so she'd give me a surname. As for my origins on my father's side, who knows? He could have been any one out of a hundred or more of her clients."

CHAPTER TEN

ROQUE moved the Doppler ultrasound probe over the man's distended abdomen. The images were transmitted to the monitor lying between him and Jewel on the woven-vine-covered floor. She couldn't see them with the screen facing away from her.

"What do you see?" she asked him as soon as he'd concluded his exam of the abdomen and moved on to the pelvis.

"Hmm, just a minute. I'm capturing more images."

When the minute became five and he still didn't answer as he clicked away on his laptop, her banked heat rose.

He'd been doing this, ignoring her, since he'd hurled the truth about his parentage at her.

For the hour it had taken to reach the Manis village, she'd shriveled with mortification, trying to imagine how it had been for him, his childhood, his struggles without the support of a family and the difficulties of his mother's situation—and failing. Could they have had more different formative years?

Then she'd tried to imagine how many hardships he'd had to endure, what level of dedication had seen him rise so far with everything possible against him—and still couldn't. It was beyond phenomenal.

She'd tried to approach him, convey all that stormed in her heart, but he hadn't let her. Then they'd reached the village, met the villagers and organized their schedule of exams and educational sessions with the tribal elders, and he'd kept treating her like he did the air around him. It had been then that her mortification had morphed into resentment.

She'd been keeping him at arm's length out of pure survival. But she *hadn't* been ignoring him. Why was he?

Did he regret telling her something so profoundly personal? Did he think she was judging him? Did he think her such a shallow, snobbish, empty shell? Still?

His unapproachable profile made her think of worst-case scenarios, made her wish she hadn't sent her team off to other cases so she was alone with him. As if he needed her support—in any way!

In another minute she gave up hope that he'd acknowledge or include her, and decided to find answers for herself.

But as he hadn't even taken the time to make introductions, it was up to her to perform them herself and, using the few indigenous words she knew, she did.

Their patient was Moie and his wife was Tuia. Tuia was as alert as her husband was lethargic, her sun-baked body naked to the waist, like the rest of the tribe, and there was a child no younger than five sleeping on her back. Patting the spot she had vacated beside her husband, she made it look as if she was carrying nothing at all as she jumped to her feet, giving Jewel the optimum place to conduct her exam. Moie squeezed his yellowed black eyes, giving her his consent to examine him.

An overall look, followed by palpating Moie's abdomen and pelvis and examining his edematous legs, told her a lot. But as he wasn't up to making the effort, she turned to Tuia and questioned her about his complaints in an elaborate set of pantomimes. The bright woman caught on with amazing accuracy, her answers bolstering Jewel's suspicions.

But when Jewel tried to ask a more complex question, she found out the limit of non-verbal communication. But even without that answer, she had her diagnosis.

She was delineating treatment in her mind when Roque finally announced his verdict. "Ascites and hepatosplenomegaly."

Oh, yeah? She could have told him that without all the gadgets. It had taken her a few palpating dips and percussion taps on Moie's abdomen to detect free fluid floating in his abdominal cavity and the hugely enlarged spleen and liver.

"And your diagnosis?" She raised her eyebrows at him.

He cocked one formidable eyebrow back at her, his eyes devoid of expression for the first time since she'd seen him again. For the first time ever. "Are *you* testing *me* now?"

Her heart constricted. *Keep it light.* She did. "Yep, since you're on my turf. This case is pure internal medicine."

"You mean *you* have a diagnosis?" At her nod, his eyebrows drew together into a forbidding glower. "Don't you mean a *differential* diagnosis?"

She shook her head, ignored the itch behind her sternum that his uncharacteristic harshness inflicted. "That's the problem with you surgeons. You can't consider coming up with a diagnosis without using all your gadgets on the patient. We internists rely on good old case histories and examination."

"And that's why you're often wrong, as evidenced by the ever-increasing numbers of your chronic patients! And God only knows how many people you actually kill, slowly or quickly, never even realizing it. Then you pat yourselves on the back and go have lunch! Symptoms can overlap from one relatively benign condition to another catastrophic one, and your so-called history taking and exams are never enough to make the distinction. I question your unsubstantiated instincts and self-satisfied diagnostic skills and the way you approach a patient with your human limitations and prejudices. These often blind you to the obvious until it's too late. 'Gadgets,' on the other hand, don't have opinions or preconceptions—and they certainly don't have egos!"

An unbearable pressure built behind her eye sockets. Her heart battered her ribs until it shook her whole body, until it felt pulped. So that was how it felt to be really exposed to his wrath. Where did it come from? Was that how he saw her? Or…

Her streaking, stricken thoughts came to a stuttering halt when his eyes squeezed shut. His teeth made a bone-scraping sound as he shredded a string of murderous self-abuse.

She vaguely felt Tuia fidgeting behind her and Moie growing restless. Roque had kept his voice level, his face impassive as he'd delivered his razing summation, but his aggression had been unmistakable and, to her, devastating.

He lowered his head and a bass, shaken groan escaped him. "*Jewel—perdoe-me… Deus!*" His eyes suddenly rose to hers, black now, shimmering. Their impact punched her breath out. "But how can I ask you to forgive me? That was unforgivable—and nothing to do with you. Believe me, Jewel, forgive me, please…"

His gaze fell again and, moved beyond endurance, she reached out and cupped his cheek. His hand immediately covered hers, his lips turning into her palm in a beseeching kiss that should have burned through it. But it wasn't that that succeeded in bringing the tears she hadn't shed in all her ordeals. It was the naked pain in his eyes.

He spoke, his lips still in her palm, his subdued words vibrating in her flesh, booming in her bones. "It was my mother… She was visiting so-called friends, a huge sentimental mistake I tried everything to stop her from making. The town knew what she'd once done for a living and when she fell sick, the doctors assumed fever and consciousness disturbance were an exacerbation of an untreated venereal disease. They started her on antibiotics, antipyretics and sedatives. By the time they suspected their unsubstantiated diagnosis and did an ECG, her myocardial infarction had destroyed most of the cardiac muscle. They called me then. I arrived in time for her last breath."

Oh, God. Oh, *God*.

It was all she could do, for their audience's benefit, to crush back a distressed wail and the urge to envelop him in a frantic hug, to absorb his anguish into herself.

This man she'd married and left, never suspecting how incredible he was, how unique. That he wasn't ashamed of his mother, that he hadn't judged or blamed her said volumes. Another man would have writhed for ever in a misogynistic hell, damaged and nurturing endless psychoses. She'd clearly been a good mother to him and he'd as clearly loved her. His unabated anguish at losing her proved just how much he had.

Then an epiphany hit her, hard. Was losing his mother through the prejudice and negligence of other doctors what drove him? Was he saving her in every patient he treated? No wonder he'd come running when he'd suspected she was a prima donna who was only playing doctor, to protect his people from her incompetence. And considering what he'd suffered through most of his life, it was amazing he'd had that much control and grace, dealing with *her* deliberately ignorant prejudices.

Her hand was still pressed to his cheek. She was enervated

by emotion. But she just had to tell him, she had to…how much…how much…

"I can't tell you how sorry I am for your loss, Roque," she choked. "I wish you'd told me before…"

He held her streaming eyes for an endless moment then pressed another kiss into her palm, thankful, apologetic, the fever pitch of emotion leveling. He wiped away her tears, his fingers gentle, cherishing. "*Obrigado, Jóia,* for making me wish I had."

With that he turned to Moie and Tuia and made profuse apologies in every indigenous and sign language he knew. Then he turned to her and his smile almost knocked her heart out of her.

"You were going to tell me your diagnosis?" he purred.

She recovered with every iota of control she had and mumbled, "Are you asking for it so you can knock it?"

"I wouldn't dare." His eyes sobered and the sincerity in them buffeted her. "I'm truly sorry about that outburst, Jewel. I'd be more than an idiot to belittle your skills. You were right. As a surgeon my clinical powers lie elsewhere. I have differential diagnoses that need more tests to settle on one. But *you've* settled on one. So tell me."

"It's—it's…" Great. Now she was stuttering. Very convincing and authoritative. She tried again, aiming for both qualities, and blurted it out instead. "It's bilharziasis."

He stared at her. She felt herself shrinking. "I think…"

After she had muttered the qualification, her prior conviction reasserted itself. The signs and symptoms were too definitive.

She tried again, with more confidence this time. "He has symptoms of both types of the flatworm infestation. Urinary-tract symptoms are painful urination with bleeding at the end.

Gastrointestinal symptoms are diarrhea, dysentery, also liver involvement, evidenced by vomiting blood, ascites, lower limb edema and enlarged liver and spleen."

Roque's smile broke out slowly and a full orchestra swelled in her ears. "Who needs gadgets when I have you?"

This man was out to kill her today!

"It fits his condition perfectly. But…" He rubbed his jaw. "The open waters of the Amazon are not known for harboring the parasite's snail host. So where could he have gotten infected?"

"I tried to ask Tuia if there's a body of water where only he went, but that was where sign language failed."

"It has to be a side-stream or a stagnant— Wait!" His hand gripped hers. "I noticed plots of land hacked out of the jungle and planted with maize. Those were flooded, perfect for the snail to live in. And only the men farm it there."

"So all the other men who also farm are probably infected."

He nodded. "But none as advanced as Moie here. That was an incredible piece of diagnosis, *bela*."

His praise left her shaking with the effort to suppress the urge to throw herself into his arms. "Wait until we make sure before you start praising my acumen, Roque."

"We'll run tests but I can't think of another diagnosis now. You cracked this one open with a touch, *amor*."

Amor. He'd been saying that constantly, in mockery, in seduction. Now it felt as if he meant it. Could it be…?

"But we have a dilemma." He seemed oblivious to her state. Or she was a better actress than she'd thought. "Bilharziasis is one thing—probably the first of many—that I didn't come prepared for. I don't expect you have any Biltricide in your pharmacy?"

Biltricide, the drug of choice, which had a 100 percent cure rate with a single oral dose, *was* stocked in their pharmacy, thanks to Inácio. She told him.

"*Maravilhoso*. I'll have to let Inácio humiliate me in another chess game in reward for his foresight. But while the drug will cure Moie's worm load, we must now treat his complications. So, *amor,* while I run tests, you tell the others to get the drug from the riverboat and educate the tribe in eradicating the snail host and preventing re-infection."

She nodded, performed her chore then hurried back to find Roque explaining it all to Moie and Tuia. She didn't understand most of what he said, but she could tell from a few words here and there, from his expression and tone and their reactions, that in extreme care and compassion he made them understand that, though some irreversible damage had occurred, if Moie followed their instructions and didn't get re-infected, he'd improve until he could lead an almost normal life.

Then he rose and gently escorted Tuia and her still soundly asleep child out. He came back as she settled on Moie's other side, his eyes settling on her. "So—what's your treatment plan, *Jóia?*"

She cleared her emotion-clogged throat. She could tell he wasn't testing her, just reveling in this incredible alliance as much as she was.

"Diuretics for his ascites, then a TIPS procedure." This came out too breathless. "Thank God you're here to do it." And this came out too fervent.

"No other reasons to thank God I'm here?"

She tried not to give him too complete a victory, gave him a dismaying, "None." It came out too swooning.

In answer, he gave her an inscrutable look.

With a booming heart, she administered pre-procedure medications, asked, "Conscious sedation or general anesthesia?"

"You can handle general?" There was no surprise in his voice, just—wonder? She nodded, fluttering. "Let's go for concious. Better for his general condition."

Then he started the procedure and it felt so right to be assisting him, as if she'd trained all those years to that end. Was that somehow true?

The minutes passed as he performed the complicated sequence. Then he finally murmured, "Done."

And in under an hour for a procedure notorious for lasting three.

He withdrew his catheter and she jumped with a dressing to the puncture site. They continued their fluent interaction, finishing off the post-procedure care.

With Moie sleeping peacefully, she took off her surgical garb, struggled up on numb legs to rush out to Tuia with the good news. And Roque's arms caught her.

Only anticipation held her up as he captured her head in both hands. He groaned her name, moved feverish fingers and eyes over her eyelids and lips, and her knees melted.

He ravaged her senses just being near him. Then he took her lips. With the voracity of a predator unleashed on a prey that had been long kept an inch out of reach. With the cherishing of a man fearing for his only sustenance in life.

When her whimpering became incessant, he severed the deep kiss on a frustrated snarl, kept mashing their lips together as he rasped, "*Senhora* Da Costa, we must do this together often. Very, very often."

CHAPTER ELEVEN

WHAT *was* "this?"

Roque's statement had been revolving in her mind since they'd been invited to stay at the Manis village three days ago.

Had "this" meant working together? Or was "this" that soul-shattering kiss afterwards? If he'd meant the latter, inflaming her, giving her glimpses of heaven then stepping back and leaving her stumbling back into hell, he could forget it.

And it seemed he had. There'd been many almosts and nearlys since, but no repeat performance. Certainly no follow-up.

She felt as if he was waiting for something. Some sign from her? What more signs could she give him? She'd *told* him how much she wanted him, *after* he'd walked away, saying not now, spouting inexplicable stuff. Then she'd stepped back, too, deciding to give up rather than shrivel in the torment of his baffling decrees of courtship and anticipation, and he'd snared her again, got her to admit in surrender louder than words that she was his for the taking. And he'd stepped away again.

He *had* to be taking his revenge. What else explained his maddening behavioral yo-yo? Though it was still incredible just working and interacting with him, she was so raw by now she felt that if he so much as looked at her she'd bolt.

He was looking at her now as he entered their vaccination tent. He was always looking at her. She didn't bolt. She never did. She couldn't miss one second of the heart-pulping intensity and poignancy of anything she could have of him. It would soon be over anyway. Then she'd never have even that again.

He stopped by her table, wearing only shorts and an open shirt. She tried to convince her senses not to overload.

He nodded a smiling greeting at Inácio and Madeline, cast a look at their set-up, fingered her stack of vaccination cards then his gaze stopped at hers, his smile taking on an elusive quality. "You didn't join me in my morning list."

His statement was devoid of irritation, soft, almost cajoling. She wondered why because he did have reason to be irritated. She *had* said she would join him. But when Madeline had come running to her, she'd already decided to take the morning off from ambiguity and frustration. There was the afternoon list to contend with and the rest of the expedition in which to resume heartache after all, and she'd needed a break to recharge, to be able to continue in all the nerve-racking uncertainty. And then she'd known he'd handle everything alone just fine.

"Um, yeah, Madeline and Inácio ran into some big problems here and needed my assistance more." And that was also the truth. "You finished already?"

"I actually only did six cases, waiting for you to show up, then decided to see what was holding you up. I thought you'd be swamped in some other thing, so I came to help." He made an encompassing gesture with his hand. "But this place is deserted. So what's going on? Where are your patients?"

She gave him what she hoped was a serene look. "Hiding.

Horror tales have spread about the torture we're inflicting here and its consequences."

Madeline gave an exaggerated sigh. "Yeah, we thought you left us the easy chore when you turned vaccination over to us. Little did we know, eh? First the tongue-lolling struggle to convince the elders yesterday that sticking needles into the healthy is to protect them from catching possibly fatal diseases from newcomers. Then they ordered everyone to brave our needles—*not* that *brave* is the right word here. You'd think we were killing them, for all the hassle they gave us."

Inácio nodded in resignation. "We managed to vaccinate sixty out of a projected three hundred. Then this morning they converged here again, agitated, and we burned up Montoya's translation software to convince them that inflammation of the injection site is a normal reaction, and that fever, malaise, muscle aches and other systemic symptoms are natural, especially as they've never been exposed to the antigens, and that symptoms will be gone in a couple of days."

"Sounds you were doing just fine so far," Roque commented. "Where's the but?"

Madeline exhaled. "Yeah, a very big but. As soon as they succumbed and agreed to continue with the vaccination, the first villager we vaccinated, and a strapping man he was, had that damned one in half a million anaphylactic reaction. I left Inácio with him and ran to fetch Jewel."

Concern leapt in his eyes as they turned on Jewel. "Why didn't you come for me?"

"I would have if I'd had any doubt I couldn't handle it," Jewel said defensively. "And if I didn't know your were already deep in a procedure by then. But even after the man was OK, everyone ran into hiding and wouldn't come out no matter how much we begged. I sent Montoya on what is looking like mission impossible to convince them into giving it another shot—if you'll pardon the pun—and bringing the kids along for the fun. He's been gone an hour now. I'm beginning to think we shouldn't hold our breath."

Suddenly the weird watchfulness in Roque's gaze evaporated, mischief flooding in its wake. "What would you give me if I got them all in here, in line, ready to take their vaccines with a smile and a thank you?"

"For that miracle? Anything! What would you want?"

"You know what I want." Did she, now? Was he kidding? She knew nothing! The look in his eyes became even more bone-melting. "And under no circumstances are you not joining me for the afternoon list, or not coming to me in any crisis from here on." He bent, took her twisting lips in a hot kiss then straightened and winked at her. "Give me ten minutes."

He strode out of the tent, leaving her mute, Madeline fanning herself and Inácio chuckling and shaking his head.

She remained staring after him as Madeline and Inácio ribbed her, discussed her and Roque's relationship openly, gave theories and predictions, until she growled, "Oh, shut up!"

It only made them worse.

At the end of the promised ten minutes, Roque re-entered the tent with a flourish. "Milady, your patients are queuing for your favors."

She got up on elastic legs, stumbled outside to see this miracle for herself and, sure enough, there they were, dozens and dozens of men, women and children, looking at her as if she were a monster. She bet everyone who was unvaccinated in the village was accounted for.

She looked up at him, eyes wide in wonder. "Whew, that was short work. Just how did you get them here?"

His lips twisted. "You expect me to reveal my secrets?"

God forbid. "OK, be inscrutable. But do it while making yourself even more useful. Let's start with the worst. Get the men in first. Tell them it makes them great role models."

He traced a lazy finger down her exposed arm. "As long as I end up getting what I want." Then he turned around, leaving her wondering where the oxygen in the atmosphere had gone.

She staggered back to her table, growled another "Shut up" at Madeline and Inácio.

"But we haven't said anything!" Madeline protested.

"You're thinking it loud and clear. Whatever it is. And I don't want to hear it. Now, hop to it. Ready groups of twenty at a time. Let's give each person everything at once. DPT, pneumococcal, hepatitis A and B, MMR, chickenpox and meningococcal. Add the oral polio vaccine for the kids."

"Yes, boss." Inácio gave a mock bow as he opened their battery-operated fridge and extracted vials of vaccines and dilutents while Madeline readied dozens of syringes.

Roque walked in with the first ten men. "You're giving them the full treatment? No wonder the vanguard ran screaming."

"In fact, I made the mistake of giving Maddy and Inácio instructions to give them only part of the vaccination regimen, and it only made those partially vaccinated even more reluctant patients. But a lesson has been learned. These people won't know what hit them. Wham, wham and wham and it's over."

"Shock therapy, eh? *Sim*, it's probably best not to prolong the conflict." Roque came to stand beside her, beckoned to the first man. "It's enough that I'll tell them later I'll be sending other expeditions in time for their booster doses."

"Not a word about it now. They may refuse to go through with it if they know there'll be more jabs down the line!"

He only chuckled as the first villager, a young man with

slashed cheekbones and nervous slanting black eyes, came forward.

Jewel rose, smiled at him brightly as she cleaned his skin with an antiseptic solution then gently pinched his deltoid in one hand, murmuring encouragement to him all the time. Then she administered the first shot. His eyes widened at the sight and feel of the needle sinking into his flesh. Then he dropped unconscious at her feet.

She exclaimed in dismay as she and Roque swooped down to scoop him up and support him as he revived from his faint into one of the folding chairs. An uproar erupted from the onlookers behind them, the agitation building until Roque swung around and snapped something, then it died down.

Then he turned to her. "Fill four syringes with saline. Four-inch needles, 14-gauge."

Inácio and Madeline jumped to fulfill his demand. There was no doubt they considered him their overall boss. Oh, well. Where was the surprise?

They were done in under a minute and handed him the demanded syringes. He handed them to her then led her by the hand outside where the rest of the villagers were warily fidgeting and loudly speculating on the disturbance.

He made sure he had everyone's attention then he took off his shirt, looked down on her and murmured, "Do it to me."

Her heart fired. She realized at once what he meant. But had he also meant the *double entendre?*

Her hands clutched the syringes, leashing in the emotions roaring through her.

He made a theatrical gesture to the gawking villagers and said something that she was sure meant, "Now I'll show you how I take far bigger needles than the measly ones you're so afraid of—with a smile."

"Time to make an example out of you," she murmured, holding his eyes as she took the cover off one needle. Then her gaze moved to his deltoid as she repeated the sequence she'd done with the young man. It was she who gasped when all the needle sank in. They were talking serious muscle mass here.

With her mouth drying, her eyes went up to his again as she injected the saline.

He only gave her a sweltering grin. "Ooh, do it again."

She did, in his other arm. The third one went into his thigh. He offered his buttock for the fourth, arguing that the gluteal region was the optimum site for intramuscular injections. She opted for his other thigh instead. There was no way she was seeing or touching those steel hips.

Once she'd finished, he whistled. "What are these people afraid of? Yours is the lightest touch I ever had." With that, he turned to the villagers, said something clearly challenging.

Going by the determination that flooded their gazes and stances, she could safely say that it had worked.

As they walked back inside, the young man who'd fainted pulled himself from his slouch, rose and approached her in resolute steps, offering her his arms.

She began administering one vaccine after another, ready to give any amount of soothing necessary at the first sign of discomfort. But the young man only bit down on his lip with each sting, never taking his eyes off Roque.

Roque had really gotten to him. To all of them.

Yeah, what else was new?

Four hours later, with the four of them working together, the whole village had been vaccinated.

As soon as the last mother and bawling child had left, Inácio threw himself down on his folding chair and sighed.

"We owe you big, Roque. Before you somehow brought them here and proceeded with your leading-by-example trick, I had nightmares that we'd end up hunting down then wrestling with the six hundred and fifty-eight men, women and children here to give them their shots."

Madeline disposed of the last syringes, turned around with an exuberant smile. "Yeah. This 'do it to yourself first and dare them into taking it as boldly as you took it' sure worked."

Roque smiled back as he came to stand in front of Jewel. "Seems I did my part." He took her hands in a gentle grip. "How about doing yours?"

She pulled her hands from between his as if he'd burned her, words tumbling out. "As if you helped us in return for my assistance in the afternoon list!"

"I didn't? Why did I, then?"

"Because you're a big softie and you'd do everything if you could be in multiple places simultaneously. As for me, assisting you isn't payback. It's a reward and a huge learning opportunity. Anyone would *pay* to assist you. Now I know why medical people the world around do just that, and pay big time."

In answer, there was only this still look in his eyes as he followed her out of the tent and to their makeshift OR. And something else. Disappointment?

Yeah, sure. She was only seeing her own emotions reflected in his eyes.

But there had been only truth in her words when she'd told him how much she loved working with him. And for the next four days, as they stayed in Manis, and for the remainder of the projected eight weeks of their expedition, there would be plenty of that. It would have to be enough.

* * *

Jewel had had enough.

Something had to happen or she'd shatter with the building pressure. Mercifully, something *was* about to happen.

They were finally leaving Manis.

Workwise, their stay had been a success by all measures.

They'd examined the whole tribe, run every relevant test on all who'd needed them, administered treatments and vaccinations, done dozens of surgical procedures and followed them up, done tutorials about all possible diseases, physical and otherwise, that modern men could bring. And she'd loved each and every moment she'd spent doing all of the above. With Roque.

And the evenings spent among the generous tribe had been fantastic. The females had flocked around her and Madeline, unable to get enough of examining the gold that was Madeline's hair, the pieces of sky in her eyes. They found Jewel as mesmerizing even if her coloring wasn't as exotic to them. Mostly they were awed by her height. And far more so by her man's, as they referred to Roque. As everyone referred to him.

That had only made things worse. For he wasn't her man. He was just…just… She had no idea what he was, what he wanted to be. Or what *she* wanted him to be.

Then had come the nights. She'd known nights filled with pain, despair and isolation. Nothing else had ever felt like that.

She'd spent those nights with Madeline in the hut of a fatherless family. Their hostesses had been delighted and delightful but they could have been torturing her for all the enjoyment she'd derived from their company and attention. She'd spent the hours till dawn aching in oppression and frustration.

And now they were at last returning to their boats to head to their next destination. Once on board, would he…?

Her thoughts shattered at the sight of men running, converging on them, wielding spears and blowguns, quivers swinging on their backs. That sure didn't look like a farewell party, more like a hunting one. What was going on?

Madeline sauntered towards her. "Of all the chauvinistic rubbish! They're going hunting and no women allowed!"

Inácio came to stand beside them. "No *one* allowed, Maddy. This is their most sacred hunt, to bring sacrifices to thank their gods—this time for bringing us here. It's a privilege and responsibility reserved for the Manis warriors."

"But Roque is going," Madeline complained. "Since when did he become a Manis warrior?"

"Roque is the leader of those they're thanking their gods for," Inácio supplied with a complacent insider's attitude. "Nothing less could have made them transgress their tribal laws. And he won't be allowed to join the hunt or wield a weapon. Just accompanying them is their highest honor."

Roque going out there in the jungle where boa constrictors and jaguars roamed? Unarmed?

She didn't think so.

"You're *not* going hunting."

Jewel's whisper struck Roque's every sensitized nerve. He swung around. He was way beyond the end of his tether and almost afraid of the moment he had her alone. He forced himself under control, smiled. "I'm not, *amor*. I'm going to watch."

"That's even worse. And you're not doing it."

Could it possibly be she was worried about him? He savored the pleasure of the fantasy as he said, "I'm a big boy. Very big. Even a jaguar wouldn't pick me to maul to death, *Jóia*. And I can't not go. It would be too great an insult."

"Fine. Then I'll go with you."

His heart swelled. She was worried about him, thought there was danger out there and wouldn't let him go alone into it!

He struggled to articulate anything, his voice alien in his own ears when he did, quavering with elation. "It may be ridiculous to us, but women aren't allowed on hunts here."

"I'm not a woman."

The ridiculously far-fetched assertion brought a guffaw tearing from his gut. "*Jóia*, if you were any more of a woman I would have died of a feminine overdose long ago. I'm constantly teetering on the brink as it is."

Her golden eyes flared that lethal womanliness. "I'm *not* a woman here, I'm the leader, too. And that's why *you're* going."

With that she swung around, dragged Montoya in her wake, swooped down on the tribe's elders and had him scrambling to translate what an insult it would be for them to leave her out of this, that they were honor-bound to respect *their* culture.

All through he watched, rapt.

He wouldn't have believed he could get more delighted with her, this assertive, addictive Amazon that she'd become. But he was. And he loved it. And her…?

No. Love had been an illusion and it was in the past. This hunger, this was real, this was here and now. And at the first moment possible, he was going to assuage it.

Jewel felt nauseous.

Not only because she was about to witness an animal being slaughtered but also because she'd dropped her last shield.

The panic that had suffocated her at the thought of Roque in danger had forced a devastating admission that had left her insides exposed. She was falling in love with him.

Falling? Still struggling for a survival strategy, wasn't she? Like she'd been doing since she'd first seen him.

She'd long fallen. Utterly. Irrevocably. And it *hurt*.

Something inside her, blindly hopeful, kept pleading, What could be better than to fall in love with your own husband?

Everything else answered, What could be worse?

She couldn't be his wife. Even if he wanted her to be. Which he didn't. Thank God. For him. For her, she had no idea how she would survive the pain—if she could survive it…

A movement mercifully suspended her desperate thoughts. The prey was in sight. And it had to be a deer, didn't it?

The whitetail deer lowered its head to nibble at some leaves. Pity swelled in her gut. Heaven knew, she was no vegetarian, but witnessing the extermination of a life! But she couldn't have let Roque come alone. The jungle had too many dangers. She had to make sure he was safe, in her sights, within her reach. She now reached back for him and—*he wasn't there.*

She swung around, her frantic eyes slamming around the dense forest.

She'd lost him.

Like the damned idiot she was, she'd wandered off in a fugue and *lost* him.

She had to find him, fast. She'd clutch him to her side this time, keep him with her, safe…

A spear hurtled out of nowhere from the periphery of her vision, missing the deer. As it bolted, a storm of spears followed it, going wide.

Then she heard Roque's roar.

Panic detonated in her head. It congealed her blood, filled her lungs, spurted from her eyes and mouth.

Roque. Spears impacting him, ripping his flesh, crushing his bones… Roque, in so much agony he prayed for the mercy of instant death…like she'd once prayed…

A shriek rent her.

CHAPTER TWELVE

"JEWEL—*Jewel!*"

Roque heard the crazed shouts, barely recognized that they were issuing from him.

He'd focused on the deer for seconds and had turned to find Jewel gone. The same moment they'd started throwing spears.

Dread had erupted on a bellow for them to stop. Then her shriek had torn through him and the images that had deluged his mind…! Jewel—her precious body ripped and broken, again…

Deus, Deus—no, no, no.

He hadn't dropped dead only because he had to get to her, save her.

"*Jewel.*" He bellowed again as he bounded on the stony ground, each thud threatening to dismantle him bone from bone. Then he cleared a thick thatch of ferns and saw her, standing, staggering, just twenty feet away. He had no voice left to scream her name, no mind to process the panic. Only momentum took him to her, made him turn her with flailing hands and crazed eyes—and he almost keeled over. *She was uninjured.*

And she launched herself at him, her weeping only intensifying as she smothered it in his chest.

Deus, what could he do? If only there was a threat to fight, to protect her, to stem her anguish. And what had brought it on? What was wrong? It wasn't like her to fall apart like that. Or was it? What did he really know about her?

Plenty. In the lifetime of the last three weeks he'd come to know her, the new her, better than he'd ever known anyone. So what traumas did she harbor that could make her react that way?

"*Meu amor,* I implore you, look at me…" He tried to loosen her hold, to bring her face up, and her fingers turned to talons, digging frantically into him.

His throat closed on thorns, and tears, unknown all but once, at his mother's deathbed, forced their way through his eyes.

He crushed her to him, warding off the world. "Nothing can touch you, *amor.* I'm here and I'm never leaving you…" He gestured to the milling tribesmen to leave them, to take away the deer's carcass, removing further provocation from her sight.

She finally stopped shuddering and whimpering, stood limp and quiescent within the cloak of his body. And he had to face it. Why her distress destroyed him, why her desertion nearly had. What he'd known from the first time he'd seen her.

Whether she wanted him, wanted him for a while or didn't want him at all, he was hers. For life. And probably beyond.

"I'm sorry."

Her tremulous words jolted through him. He moved away just enough to look down at her, scared she'd spiral back into anguish if he loosened his hold.

She moved, too, sniffed again. "I'm sorry."

He pressed her back to his heart in relief. "Don't be, you're all right now." Urgent fingers beneath her chin raised her face to his to make sure of his verdict. Tension rushed out at seeing her eyes clear again, at least of the terror that had tainted them. They were puffy and slumberous and he couldn't believe they had the power to arouse him to that pitch even now.

A ragged sigh escaped her and she rested her head on his heart again. "You must think I'm a nutcase."

"Why would I think you're a case of nuts?"

Her eyes snapped to his, startled. Then she laughed. *Deus,* she *laughed.*

He stroked her cheek, absorbed the inner exquisiteness that had always been her power over him. He needed to know what had provoked her panic. But he'd go to his grave content never to know. He couldn't risk stirring up her turmoil again.

She rubbed her face over his chest, still chuckling, and his heart tried to burst out of its confines to get a direct rub of her velvet cheek. "Now you must think I'm really fit for a strait-jacket." She beamed up at him. "Howling like a wounded wolf one minute and a demented hyena the next."

His smile shook on his lips as he rasped, "If you promise no more howls like the first one, howl like the second any time."

She leaned back in his arms, her hand and eyes wavering over his face. "I couldn't find you, then I heard you shout, thought they'd hit you— Oh, Roque…"

So all this had been fear for him? Could it be?

He found it hard to believe it had all been about him. So maybe something had triggered her—

Suddenly realization crushed down on him. Her accident. That had to be it. Her fear of him being accidentally injured, even killed must have resurrected her near-death experience. And he'd wondered what trauma she'd harbored! How insensitive and stupid and oblivious could he be?

"Did you—did it bring back your—your accident?" He could almost have cut his tongue off for putting his doubts into words.

Her eyes widened, as if she, too, hadn't made the connection. Her words were slow and ponderous when she said, "No. I'm long over that. I remember so clearly what streaked in my mind during those moments—there were images of every injury I've seen and treated, imagining them happening to you…" She shuddered, clung to him harder, her fingers kneading agitated patterns into his chest muscles. "I never cried like this. Not when I thought I might never walk again, or when constant pain made me wish I'd die and get it over with. Not even when everything I had and was, had gone and I knew no one would even notice if I followed."

Agony clamped his chest, kicked in his back. Was he having a heart attack? It wouldn't be strange. For how could his heart withstand that insight into the depth of her ordeal? Knowing that he'd been there, at the height of her need, and hadn't grasped it, hadn't done anything about it?

But he'd tried everything he could. And she'd refused it!

And it shouldn't have stopped him. He should have *made* her take his strength when she'd had none, and no one.

But he had *done that. He'd pushed aside her protests, loved her, married her so he could be her strength and support.*

When it had been much too late, when the damage had already carved its indelible scars in her soul. What a fool he'd been.

She turned in his arms, smoothed his drenched shirt. "I drowned you. Who needs a tropical shower with me around, huh?"

"I'd drown in your tears—I'd drown for real, if it would make you feel better, *amor.* I'm yours to do with as you please."

Moisture appeared in her eyes again, shimmered in the rays of sunshine streaming through the canopy of foliage high above them. But her smile trembled on lips beginning to flush with returning vigor and equilibrium. "Oh, darling, thank you for saying that!"

Darling. She'd never called him that, never assuaged his

starving heart with endearments. His heart clamped an obsessive fist around this one, hoarding it for fear there'd be no more.

Her hand slid a hesitant path between his shirt buttons, came to a quivering rest over his heart. "And are you sure about this generous offer? I can do with you *anything* I please?"

His throat closed. "Anything, *amor.* Anything at all."

"You won't say 'not now'…?" The last two words wobbled.

Did she mean—? Did she want…? Here? Now? He searched her face, found confirmation in eyes that had become embers, burning with a need as huge as his. *Sim, sim,* here, now. At last.

He drove trembling fingers through her hair, cupped her precious head. "I can't say 'not now'. Not if I want to live…"

Her cry tore through him when their lips collided. He could only grind his lips against hers, no finesse, no restraint. The need to hide her inside him drove him to press his all against all of hers. Incessant moans filled his head, high and deep, his and hers, as if in profound suffering. And he was—in agony. Her flesh buzzed beneath his burning hands.

"Darling—*please.* I waited long enough."

Darling—again. *Deus,* what he felt—he'd been afraid of this. He had no experience with wanting this much. He could hurt her, or leave her unsatisfied.

No. He'd die before he hurt her. He'd live to satisfy her. "*Sim amor,* longer than bearable."

She writhed out of his arms, slid down to the forest floor and onto her back, inviting him. Alarm flashed in his mind. The ground was rough, jagged—he could bruise her back.

He went down beside her, tried to raise her and she grabbed his hands on a whimper and sank her teeth into them, suckled his fingers. A growled *"Misericórdia…"* tore out of him.

She showed him no mercy, pressed his hands to her breasts, hard, shaking harder. His hands felt unmatched as he uncovered her precious flesh, as he felt the pressure to demolish their barriers, purple bursts crowding his vision. *Deus*—was he having a stroke?

Not before he gave her what she needed. But it had been so long without her—so long… He raised her, bent her over his arm and she arched in a tight bow, her breasts a desperate offering, her hands behind his head, her talons sinking in his control, speeding his descent into oblivion.

His mouth opened on her engorged flesh, took as much as he could of her matured femininity, savoring her feel and taste. He rid her of her pants in uncoordinated moves. She thrashed, helped him, her moans becoming deeper. His own urgency deepened and he reached between her legs, opened her folds and shook, on the brink, just gliding his fingers over her fluid heat. Needing to know the extent of her need for him, he slid two fingers inside her slick tightness. He went blind with the acuteness of her response, with the blast of heat and hunger—and realization.

He couldn't make love to her!

The blow was so hard he barely felt her going rigid, pushing at his hand, rasping, "I want *you*…"

He subdued her, drew harder on her nipple, thrust his fingers deeper, his thumb rubbing shaking circles over the knot of flesh where her nerves converged. He felt her convulse, gritted his teeth, anxious for the music of her release, hoping he wouldn't suffer permanent damage hearing it.

But she wasn't climaxing. She was pushing him away.

She staggered up to her knees, magnificent, disheveled—and in tears again. "You're…toying with me—again."

He barked something that was both incredulous laugh and agonized grunt. "If you think so and want to kill me for it, don't bother. I'll die any minute now."

Twin tears streaked down crimson-flushed cheeks. "But it's w-worse now. You lied this time—promised anything…"

"I promised what I can't deliver. I have no protection…"

Her gasp interrupted his impeded explanation, her eyes flooding with such stricken shock that words poured from him under pressure. "I'll get plenty from the pharmacy, make love to you all day and all night—but let me pleasure you now."

She shook her head, hiccupped a sob, her eyes full of an emotion that seared him even though he didn't understand it. What was it? Regret? Grief? Despair? All? *Deus, why?*

An endless moment of confusion and oppression passed before she whispered, "That's the only reason?" she choked again.

He drew in a shearing inhalation, nodded. And her smile broke out. His confusion only mounted at its melancholy.

Then he heard her whimpering that they didn't need protection. From then on he felt nothing but her rubbing against him, his clothes coming undone, her doing or his or both, he had no idea. Anticipation was so brutal his grip on consciousness was softening.

He fought back to focus as he sat down in the lotus position, held her eyes as he opened her thighs, locked her legs around his hips. He gritted his teeth as her moist heat singed his erection, waited for her to sink down on him, to take him.

But she didn't. She unlocked her legs and swayed up on shaking thighs, her hair swinging a thousand shades of amber and russet in the streaming rays, her breasts heaving, her face taut, her lips quivering.

She had to be punishing him. For not falling to his knees and groveling for all she had to give the moment she offered it.

He gazed his torment into her filling eyes and she swayed down for a desperate kiss, broke it only to close febrile lips over his ear. He roared. Her whisper was as intense, pouring right into his brain. "You once promised to please me until I'm mad—until I'm finished. Drive me mad, Roque—finish me."

He couldn't let her finish. He drove up into her, incoherent, invading her all the way, overstretching her scorching, living honey. And she engulfed him back, consumed him in clenching hunger, wrung him, razed him. At last. *At last.*

He rested in her depths, overwhelmed, transported, listening to her delirium, to his. Her graceful back was a deep arch, letting him do it all to her, fulfill his pledge. Blind, out of his mind, he lifted her, filled savage mouth and hands with her flesh. He withdrew all the way out of her then thrust back, fierce and full, riding her wild cry.

It took no more than that. One thrust made her complete. And him. Her satin screams echoed his roars, her body convulsed along with his in a paroxysm of release, one sustained seizure that destroyed the world around them.

Then it was another life, another time where nothing existed. Only being merged with her, still rocking together, riding the aftershocks, still pouring himself into her, feeling her around him, inside and out, sharing the descent from heaven to an even more blissful reality. His Jewel. His joy. His.

It had been beyond control. And it had been beyond description. Everything. Yet not enough. Would anything ever be?

Never. He had to have the rest of his life getting more of her, giving more of himself. All of himself. If she'd have him. *Sim*—it was way past time he faced it. His plans to have her then walk away had just been empty bravado, running scared, a desperate contingency plan in case he couldn't have her.

But he had her now. At least her desire. This time he wouldn't use it to railroad her. This time he'd let her need blossom, wouldn't follow socially imposed expectations. She'd proved to him marriage meant nothing but a piece of paper without the underpinnings of understanding, respect and trust. He wanted to be her man, no matter if he wasn't her husband. If all she wanted now were passion and freedom, he'd give them to her. Until she realized, without pressure, that he'd never tether or use her, only enrich her life and support her goals.

Her lips were pressing lightly over his face. He nuzzled her back, his hands spreading indulgence and worship over her, wallowing in delight. She melted back in the circle of his arms, humming the sound of fulfillment. His heart swelled, praying he had satisfied her as she had him. Not that he was satisfied. Would he ever be?

"Now you've finished me, what are you going to do with me?"

He couldn't believe it. His senses shot past the red zone with one sentence. He devoured her teasing right off her lips, withdrew to watch her incredible eyes going slumberous as he hardened fully inside her. "I'm going to finish you again, right now. Then I'll take you back to the riverboat and finish you again. Over and over and over again."

"Ready to be finished again?"

Jewel's grasp on the boat's railing tightened. Trembling with the effort not to swing around and throw herself in his arms, she kept unseeing eyes on the magnificent panorama they were gliding past, the tropical twilight brightening again with his nearness.

She forced out a seductive murmur in answer. "Wonder how many times you can finish me and I'll spring back re-formed."

"It's an endless process." His awesome baritone was closer, his heat almost at her back in the cooling breeze. "Didn't you read the fine print? The in-perpetuity clause?"

In perpetuity was right. It well described his presence in her thoughts, his effect on her senses and emotions.

And soon he'd snare her back into delirium. She'd lost count how many times he'd done that in the last week.

She couldn't remember much of the trip back from the hunt, just that she hadn't known what to do next, had been relieved when Roque had done it for her. He'd marched into her cabin, sought out every article of her belongings, packed them then hauled her and them all the way up to his suite. She'd been there ever since. It had been a week of indescribable ecstasy—and turmoil.

His breath now scorched her neck, then his words. "So now you understand the terms, are you ready, *meu amante?*"

His lover. He'd stopped calling her his wife. But he'd been calling her that in mockery and he'd stopped mocking her. He was beyond wonderful to her now. And he was honest. Their marriage was a forgotten piece of paper in some drawer. This was about drowning in each other, no pressure, no expectations. No future. And this was exactly what made being with him now possible.

It still didn't mean that it didn't gut her that she loved him in every way, for everything that he was and did, totally and endlessly, and he felt nothing but a passing lust for her.

She should be used to it. She'd never inspired emotions in anyone. Why should she in him? And she shouldn't wish she did for the selfish needs of her starving heart.

But knowing he would walk away, probably at the end of the expedition, sated and vindicated, was agony. It didn't make any difference that she knew this was what should happen, what she'd make sure happened, she'd still be destroyed. She was starting to crumple now.

Turn to him, tell him you want it over with now.

She turned, oppression and desperation stifling her—and almost dropped to her knees.

He was naked! For real this time. And fully, dauntingly aroused.

Her frantic gaze swung around the sundeck. A towel! She knew she'd left one on the chaise longue where they sunbathed. She streaked to it, grabbed it, threw it at him.

He just chuckled and caught her in his arms. "I'll never get used to the way you switch from wanton siren to shy prude."

"Not being an exhibitionist doesn't make me a prude." She squirmed in his arms, her gaze slamming around, ready to knock him to the deck if anyone had them in their sights.

"Me, an exhibitionist?" He gave a teasing pout. "Not at all. I just want to cut out unnecessary steps. The only undressing ritual I revel in is the one I perform on you."

"And you thought to perform it *here?*" He started to do just that, hands sliding in heavy possession and sure knowledge over her. It was like watching flames dancing closer to dynamite.

"It'll be dark in minutes." He whipped her T-shirt over her head. When had she raised her arms? Had he put her in a trance? He must have. Now he deepened it, bent to taste the flesh he'd exposed, cutting a swathe of arousal from her neck to her stomach.

And though her heart wept, her body squirmed its helpless pleasure, begged, *Just one last time.* Yes, every time had been that. Pathetic, self-destructive and she'd pay the price—later.

Logic got one last hearing. "Dark? With a tropical full moon blazing in the sky? Sure."

"What are you worried about? Some natives seeing us from the banks? As if they'd care. Or are you worried about our team, who know very well what we do here all day and all night?"

Her blood churned, inhibitions dissipating fast with every touch of friction against him. "Knowing is one thing, seeing is another."

"So you're OK with hearing? You do know they must hear us quite well in the midriver's pervasive silence, don't you?"

He laughed as she spluttered with embarrassment. Then everything ceased to matter when he took her lips in a kiss that seemed bent on extracting her soul.

He cascaded passion and possession over her, his words razing her with longing and regret, that this couldn't be real, couldn't be for ever. "I want the sky to be our only ceiling, *meu amor,* and darkness our only cover. I want to invade you, feel you capturing me and see the stars burning in your eyes, the moon gilding your beauty as I fill your every secret place, your every need, as I watch you coming undone with pleasure."

Did he mean to do it? Turning the skewer in her over and over like that? She jerked with every poignant image he painted, sank her teeth in his deltoid in her suffering.

What did she care who saw them? When their time together was over she'd never see any of their groups again. She'd leave Brazil, never to return.

She let her mind go blank, let her love and hunger bury the pain.

She watched the incredible sight of his head moving against her breasts, his lips and tongue and teeth turning them into instruments of torturing pleasure, licking and tasting and nipping wonder and hunger over their flesh before he clamped one nipple on a groan of surrender and voracity and suckling. In her receding awareness a question echoed. How could he want her?

From a long way away the answer resurfaced. She'd been fixed. That was how. All he talked about was her beauty…

All thought shut down again as he slid down her body, stripping the rest of her clothes, tormenting his way down to her toes. When he started the journey up again she was gasping in fevered snatches. "Come inside me—please—darling."

He only raised her legs over his shoulders, leaned her back against the railing, opening her core to his eyes and touch. She thrashed her protest when he probed her and blew a gust of acute sensation over her hypersensitive flesh.

"Let me feast, *meu amor.*" His ragged plea transfixed her. "I need to taste you, taste your pleasure mixed with nature." And that made her surrender everything to him. And he took it all, lapped every drop of her pleasure dry.

She tumbled from the explosive peak, lost, drained, sated, yet emptier than before, hungrier for his completion.

Her hands flailed over his lush hair, her voice no steadier when she gasped, "*Now* will you deliver on all those promises?"

He rubbed against her inner thighs, cupping her, desensitizing her. "I was waiting for your demands, for encores."

He let her melt down his shoulders and into a luxurious embrace. Then everything turned upside down as he dragged a thick mat to the deck, rolled her on it and himself on top of her in one fluid move.

He loomed over her, pressed between her eagerly spreading thighs, letting her feel his dominance for a fraught moment. Then, holding her eyes, he plunged inside her in one long thrust.

Her body jerked in profound sensual shock. At seeing the pleasure of possessing her seizing his face. At the power of the hot, vital glide of his thick, rigid shaft in her core, the reason it existed.

Her legs clamped him high over his back, giving him fuller surrender, and he ground deeper into her, until his whole length was buried inside her, filling her beyond capacity. Sensation sharpened, shredding her. She cried out, not caring who heard.

He started moving inside her, letting go of her eyes only to run fevered appreciation over her, watching as he'd said he wanted to, her every quake and grimace of pleasure. "There shouldn't be wanting like this—*pleasure* like this."

She keened and he devoured the explicit sound, his tongue invading her mouth, mimicking his body's movements inside her.

It was he who drove her crazy. The things he said, his reality, the friction and fullness of his flesh in hers, the fusion, knowing it was all she had of him, that it would end…

She cried out her desolation and his plunges grew longer, as did her cries until they merged, until she clawed at him, begged. Only then did he ride her harder, building to the jarring rhythm that would finish her, his eyes burning obsidian, his face taut with savage need, sublime in beauty in the blazing moonlight. She fought back ecstasy, greedy for the moment his seized him.

He realized, growled, "Come for me, *Jóia,* let me see what I do for you."

She thrashed her head. "Come with me…"

He roared something scalding and thrust deeper, destroyed her restraint. Release buffeted her with the force of a bursting dam, razed her body in convulsions. Those peaked to agony when he succumbed to her demand, gave her what she craved. Him, at the mercy of the ecstasy she gave him, pleasure racking him, his seed filling her in hard jets. She saw it all, felt it all, and shattered.

Time and space vanished as he melted into her, grounded the magic into reality, eased her back into her body.

Everything came back into jarring focus when he tried to

move off her. She caught him back. His weight should have been crushing, but was only anchoring.

This was what he was. Essential to her survival.

He rose on outstretched arms, his silhouette thudding in her heart, his eyes gleaming satisfaction over her ravished sight. He trailed a gently abrasive hand over her, drawled, harsh and sexy, "And tomorrow, *Jóia,* we make love under the sun."

The images pierced her as he drowned her in abandon again. Lost, she dragged him right back into delirium.

She was too weak. She couldn't end it. But she had to retrieve enough of herself to survive when it was over.

If there was anything left to retrieve…

CHAPTER THIRTEEN

"THIS looks bad."

Roque heard Madeline's mumbled assessment after she announced the woman's vitals. His heart sank. He had to agree.

As soon as they'd arrived at Aldeia Marúbo and explained who they were to the villagers, they'd been dragged to this woman's hut. He couldn't believe their timing. Another hour and Matcha would have died. She could still very well die.

His troubled gaze moved to her four children huddled in a corner of the hut. He clamped his jaw. They could lose their mother.

Inferno—no. Not on his watch. And they shouldn't be watching their mother writhing in agony either.

"Inácio," he rasped. "Get the kids out. And tell everyone to stay out."

Inácio did so, came back in a minute as Jewel initiated resuscitation measures with Madeline. Roque held back, knowing they had first claim on the patient. Matcha was in deep shock. Treating her severe hypotension was the most important thing to tackle if she was to stabilize enough to withstand their diagnostic and treatment measures.

They finished resuscitation then Jewel started her exam.

"What's your opinion?" Inácio asked tense minutes later.

Jewel continued palpating the woman's abdomen and pelvis. "From Montoya's translations of witness reports, she had sudden lower abdominal pain, vomited, lost consciousness. When she came to she couldn't move because of pain. She's now almost unconscious with depletion and shock. Other signs are tense abdomen, guarding, rebound…"

"That's all ruptured appendix signs!" Madeline exclaimed.

Jewel didn't answer, put on gloves and performed a vaginal exam, then a bimanual pelvic one. Then she sat back on her heels and announced her diagnosis. "She has placental abruption."

Roque's eyes snapped wide at her steady verdict. "Without vaginal bleeding? And we weren't even told she was pregnant."

Jewel's eyes swung to him. "Twenty percent of placental separation cases occur with concealed hemorrhage behind the placenta. And with her size, a twenty-something-week pregnancy could go unnoticed. And she might not have told anyone she was pregnant. I doubt they make much of pregnancies here."

What was that bleak shadow that flitted in her eyes? Was she remembering her own pregnancy? That she hadn't made much of it either? Was she regretting that now? *Stop it. Focus.*

He did, heard Madeline suggesting alternatives. "Couldn't it be other stuff causing acute abdomen? Intestinal obstruction, ovarian torsion, severe endometriosis—even ectopic pregnancy?"

Jewel's elegant eyebrows puckered in consideration. Then she shook her head. "No. None of these cause such severe hypotension, which can only indicate severe internal bleeding. Anyway, an ultrasound scan will tell for sure."

Jewel looked at Roque and he moved forward, trying to pin that expression in her eyes, to understand it, and why it scared him so much. She snatched it out of his reach when she turned her eyes away. He had to, too, to get on with his job.

He forced himself to block her out, moved his ultrasound probe over the woman's abdomen, watching the images with Jewel. In a minute they both let out heavy exhalations.

"So what's the diagnosis?" said Inácio.

"Ultrasound just confirmed Jewel's clinical diagnosis—a fetus, a girl, distressed but alive, around twenty-two weeks and about three pounds. And there's massive hemorrhage beneath the placenta." He turned to Jewel. "I was praying you might be wrong just this once. I was hoping this was something I had more experience with. She'll need an immediate Cesarean section."

"What about the baby?" Madeline asked.

Roque exhaled again. "We can only hope she's viable, but the mother is our priority now."

Inácio looked around the hut, clearly calculating the possible catastrophic consequences of performing major abdominal surgery here. "Can't we at least move her to the boat?"

Roque again answered him. "I doubt she'd last the two-hour trip. We have to operate, now or never."

Jewel bit her lip. "I only ever helped in a couple of Cesarean sections during my Ob-Gyn rotation."

Roque gave a grim nod. "Ob-Gyn almost slipped the net of my experience, too. But I bet we can manage it together."

Her eyes flared, then darkened. His nerves jangled.

What was that? That immense something he saw before this weird bleakness extinguished her eyes again? Was that something love? If so, why the bleakness?

Jewel tore her eyes away and turned to Inácio and Madeline, rushed to prepare their patient for the emergency C-section.

Roque had to force air into his lungs, had to will his heart to beat.

Was what he'd just seen even real? Or just his feverish hopes superimposed on her expressions? He'd been clinging to his resolution to never rush her again, but he knew he'd never survive losing her again. Not knowing if she might consider making their relationship real, permanent this time, was fraying his stamina. So much so he was beginning to consider ending it. If she couldn't love him, he should walk away before uncertainty destroyed his mind, drove him to unpredictable behavior.

But he hadn't imagined that look in her eyes! Or any other ever since they'd become lovers again. Yet how could it be what he hoped, when it was followed by such despondency? Didn't she want to love him? Did she still think him beneath her? Was that why she didn't want to admit it, to him, to herself?

Stop it. Drive yourself crazy later. See to your patient.

He turned to Madeline as she and Inácio swooped on him and Jewel, scrubbing and gowning them, then draping Matcha, leaving only the surgical field exposed. Then he and Jewel worked together, initiating general anesthesia.

He took his position by the patient's right side and Jewel immediately took his assistant's position, handing him a scalpel. He met her eyes above her mask. They were impassive now. He crushed down the spurt of anxiety, turned his eyes to the surgical field and made a low transverse incision.

He explained his decision. "A midline incision provides quicker access to the uterus but a transverse one carries less risks post-operatively and will provide us with better pelvic visualization."

She only nodded, helped him extend the incision and deepen it. Once they entered the peritoneal cavity she placed retractors, grasped the loose peritoneum with forceps for him to incise, was ready with a bladder blade to both protect the bladder and provide exposure of the lower uterus.

Their eyes met again for a bolstering moment before he opened the uterus, extending the incision with his index finger, holding his breath at the unaccustomed procedure, until the fetal membranes were revealed. He cut through them and heard Jewel's sharp gasp. He snapped a look up, found her trembling, her gaze transfixed on the tiny legs he'd exposed.

His heart battered his ribs, at her distress, at the scary sight of the fragile life, at the enormous responsibility. He gritted his teeth, hating to ask this of Jewel. But there was no other way. "Jewel, I need you to take care of the baby once I deliver it. I must devote all I have to the mother."

Jewel jerked her head in a vigorous nod. He couldn't spare her another second as he delivered the terrifyingly small girl, handed her to Jewel, double-clamped the umbilical cord and cut it. Then he forgot all about Jewel and the rest as he fought to stem the catastrophic hemorrhage once the placenta released the accumulated blood behind it.

Then he found Jewel fighting beside him again, cauterizing bleeding vessels, suctioning blood, while Inácio and Madeline struggled to keep up with their demands. But nothing was enough. Then the woman flatlined. They dragged her from death's clutches and fought on. But Roque knew there was only one solution.

"I have to do a hysterectomy." Jewel's eyes slammed into him. He rushed to justify his decision, to try to wipe away her stricken look. "It's the only way to stem the hemorrhage, and she already has four—five children, if this baby lives."

She lowered her reddened eyes, nodded. Then without another word or look they proceeded with the surgery of removing the enlarged, pulped uterus.

It felt like he'd run a hundred miles as he inserted the last stitch, closing the woman's skin. Then he raised his grit-filled eyes. They met Jewel's. They looked as abused as his felt. She turned away, rose and went to the baby where she'd left her.

"Inácio?" He snapped his head around, asking for a report on the patient's general condition as he followed her.

"BP 80 on 50 but holding," Inácio said.

"Get her as much blood as you can." Roque knelt beside Jewel by the tiny baby as she started checking her.

"I only suctioned her throat…" she whispered, her voice wobbling. "Checked she was breathing before I rejoined you."

He was afraid to touch the baby, his hands feeling huge and dangerous next to her spindly limbs. He didn't need to. Jewel was taking care of her. *Her* hands looked perfect, magical as she handled the flimsy little life, poured care and healing over her.

She raised cloudy eyes to him, a tremulous smile wavering on bloodless lips. "I believe she'll live. She wants to live." She lowered her gaze to the diminutive girl, gave her match-like fingers an ultra-gentle tickle. "Don't you, little one?"

His throat tightened, images, fantasies, cravings crowding his heart and imagination to bursting. Jewel—his incomparable Jewel, indulgent, proud, crooning to her baby. His baby…

She hadn't wanted his baby before. But she'd changed. Could this have changed, too? Could she want his baby now…?

He almost scoffed out loud. *Sim.* Thinking of babies before he knew if she wanted any sort of commitment at all.

But this was what a baby meant to him now. Her commitment.

Before, he'd wanted to have the family he'd never had, with her. Now he only wanted her. Babies would only be more bonds to entwine her life with his.

Madeline's hushed yet animated tones broke through his heavy-hearted musings. "She's scary—and unbelievably adorable! The horrible circumstances of her birth aside, doesn't she make you wish to have tiny living miracles like her of your own?"

Roque's whole being surged. What would Jewel say to that?

She didn't say anything, kept on working as if Madeline's question had been rhetorical.

Did she think it had been? Or was it just she didn't have an answer either way? Because she'd never thought about it, never considered it something to think about? Would he ever know how she felt about this? Would he ever work up the nerve to ask? And if he did, what would she tell him?

"Would you mind telling me where we're going?" Jewel giggled as she ran after Roque in the forest, jumping over the hurdles of heavy leaves and gnarled roots.

Roque looked back at her, his heart in a state of constant expansion. "Which part of 'it's a surprise' didn't you get?"

She stuck her tongue out at him and he laughed and stopped suddenly, breaking her momentum in an electrifying collision with his body. Momentarily startled then immediately mischievous eyes scorched him and he scooped her up in his arms, swung her round and round. He wanted to shout with delight. So he did.

"Put me down, Tarzan! You'll break your back!" she squealed, laughing harder, kicking her heels in the air.

"It would take two of you to start to be any real strain." He raised her higher until her arms were fully stretched on his shoulders. He loved the feel of her, the weight of her, the life and passion and beauty of her. He loved her.

And he was really beginning to think she loved him, too.

She laughed again, wriggled up there, looking down on him in laughing challenge. "I'll have you know I weigh 165 pounds."

"And every pound an indispensable building block in a

work of divine art, *amor*." He smiled his joy up at her. Then devilry mixed with the sublime feelings. "And if you could see what I see from here, you'd know why I may keep you up there all day."

"As if you could!" she teased.

"Let's see, shall we?" He hauled her up higher.

She yelped in delight then a hundred imps somersaulted in her incredible eyes. "Is this a challenge? All right, you're on. I say you won't be able to hold me up two more minutes!"

"And I say I'll hold you up ten. What does the winner get?"

"I suggest the loser gets a penalty."

He winked at her. "Whatever. It's a win-win situation for me. I win, I get you. I lose, you penalize me and I love it."

She crinkled her eyes at him. "You won't love the penalty. Not at first. I will, though, every delicious step of the way."

"Sounds exactly like the penalty I have in mind for you. Decadent enjoyment for me, torment for you. It will make putting you out of your misery all the more memorable."

"Ha. Prepare to lose, buddy!" She threw herself into their impromptu game, making hilarious faces at him until he burst out laughing and let her down within the two minutes she'd predicted.

"Saboteur!" He laughed as she melted down his body, reveling in the slide of her slick flesh on his, in the way she made the most of the erotic glide. Then she came to settle where she belonged, filling his arms.

He enfolded her with cherishing pressure, his insides quivering as her arms enfolded him back, as he caught tender, hungry lips all over his face before he sank his in them, over and over, drowning in their deepening connection.

She had to love him. He wouldn't feel so cherished, so welcome and appreciated, so warm and invincible when she looked at him, took him into her arms, if she didn't. She wouldn't be so responsive, so eager for everything with him, the camaraderie, the laughter, the hardships, if she didn't. She counted on him, gave him every appreciation and respect, every care and courtesy. This was way beyond passion, beyond anything he'd ever hoped for or imagined.

He stroked her cheek with his, pressed her for one more moment, sending up a prayer of humble, fervent thanks for her.

"Ah—I love winning," she purred when he finally let her go and bent to pick up the bags they'd dropped. "Does the surprise involve being someplace where I can perform my penalty on you?"

He caught her saucy lips again in a hard press, grinned at her. "I'm not saying. Keep walking and find out."

She nipped his chin then clung to his arm and fell into step with him. His eyes raked over her with heavy desire. Hers gave back as good as she got.

She was in her swimsuit, he in his. For the last week they'd rarely worn anything more, taking their dress code from their hosts. Unlike their stay in Manis, they didn't have much to do in Aldeia Marúbo. Apart from following up the post-operative Matcha and her tiny premature daughter, with the whole population only around two hundred and fifty, they'd wrapped up their work in the first two days and had had the opportunity to kick back and live life as simply as those people lived it. And it had been glorious.

Seeing how people lived in perfect harmony without any outside resources had put into perspective how they, as part of the "civilized" world, had not only become dependent on their modern props, but had become as reliant on social and interpersonal games and maneuvers and deceptions.

In the village, as there was no technology or amenities,

there were also no social or personal complexities. And this simplicity simplified his views and emotions until he forgot there were reasons to erect shields, to not open himself up and just be happy.

And he had. He'd dropped his worries and doubts and plunged into profound happiness for the very first time in his life.

And here was his happiness made flesh, snuggling into him.

He hugged her tighter to his side, groaned with overflowing emotions. "*Meu beleza,* you're beautiful—just beautiful."

He felt a tremor pass through her. He assigned a good reason to it. That was, until a few minutes later she was dispensing with his support and walking separately, and his doubts crashed down on him as if they'd never dissipated.

This had been happening ever since they'd arrived here. This episodic withdrawal. As if she sometimes caught herself doing something she shouldn't. Each time it had passed and he couldn't guess what could have triggered the dimming, the remoteness.

But couldn't he guess, or was he just scared to acknowledge that similar episodes of withdrawal had heralded the end in the past? He'd noticed them then, rationalized them, ignored them, right up until the moment she'd told him she was leaving him. It had taken five months for her to get enough of him back then. Was his novelty wearing off faster this time? Now she was older, more experienced?

If it was, it was his fault, over-eager, starving, lovesick moron that he was. He might be scaring her, overwhelming her again. Sickening her? *Deus, no.* He had to slow down, back off, remember his initial resolve, try to stick by it again.

He was pathetic. Soaring in undreamed-of heaven one moment, drowning in the dregs of unspeakable hell the next.

"Oh, wow, this has to be it!"

The awe in her voice brought him crashing back to reality. They'd arrived at their destination and he hadn't even noticed. She turned to him with a delighted smile and everything was right again. Had the world ever been anything but perfect?

He spread his arms so he wouldn't reach for her. "*Meu amor,* I give you paradise."

"Oh, Roque. I don't think even paradise can be like this." She pirouetted in abandon, a perfect Eve, tall and lush and vital.

This place was magic. A few acres of natural clearance within the dense forest, with a pond of turquoise water coming out of nowhere and every bird and butterfly on the face of the earth, it seemed, making it home.

The tribal shaman had brought him here yesterday, one medicine man to another. It was sacred ground and only shamans were allowed to come here to meld with nature and pray to the gods. He'd gotten the shaman's blessing to bring his woman, but only because, to the man's utter confusion, she was a shaman, too. He'd told him it would be the best place to get her with child. A child conceived here would be favorite of the gods.

His aching heart followed her every move as she ran here and there, exclaiming in glee, scaring the ponderous flock of herons standing on one leg in the pond.

A child. Hers. Would she ever want one again? Would it be his child she'd want? They'd been making love without protection, but she'd told him from the first day they didn't need it. She must be protected, probably by an IUD.

But why had she had one fitted? Because she'd been sexually active? Had she indulged in unprotected sex with others? *He* never had. She was the only one he'd ever trusted, the only one he'd ever shared full intimacy with. Did she go around trusting men to be conscious of their health? Had he been a fool not to take precautions for that reason alone?

His heart was stabbed with a lance of jealousy and oppression. Then she turned to him, her smile elated and again, fool that he was, everything else ceased to matter.

"Roque, did you see those?" She jumped up and down as she pointed towards one of the trees ringing the glade filled with chattering, quarreling birds. "Toucans! And those have to be macaws. And I saw hummingbirds and hawks. And about a hundred kinds of butterflies."

The last of his agitation dissipated as his lips widened indulgently. "And there are also more than two hundred species of mosquito."

"Ha—my repellant ointment laughs at all two hundred species." She walked up to him, hugged him around the waist. It took all his control not to crush her to him. "Thanks, darling. This is my life's most magnificent surprise. This place is phenomenal."

He smiled down on her, his heart constricting. "Tomorrow we go to see another phenomenon, the 'meeting of the waters'."

"I still can't believe the black, clear waters of the Rio Negro can actually run side by side without mixing with the clay-colored waters of the Rio Solimões, and for many miles."

"That's why it's called a phenomenon." He pinched her cheek when she narrowed her eyes at him, made another face and chuckled. "And then this place is more of a phenomenon than you realize. According to the shaman, places like this are magical foci, radiating fertility to the whole region. And shamans—as he considers us to be—harness their powers, use them as a nexus to the gods to bring forth bountiful sustenance—and progeny."

Suddenly he felt as if she'd been transported to another plane, leaving him behind.

This new attack of remoteness hit him the hardest ever,

shattered his resolve to cool down, to lay off. Calling himself a self-destructive, self-defeating fool, he caught her in a harder embrace. He had to stop her from drifting away. He wouldn't survive her leaving him, not again.

He devoured her lips, and with a groan that shook him she came back to him. But not completely. And he went mad.

He barely snatched a mat from his backpack, threw it on the ground before he dragged her there. She went down, no reciprocating fervor, just limp surrender.

He had to have her fire, her ardor. He had to!

He discarded their swimsuits then his hands and lips roamed her, exploited every bit of knowledge and experience with her responses and preferences, trying to ignite her. He almost wept with relief when she caught fire at last and gasped for him.

He covered her body, thrust inside her, maddened, as if he'd stamp her with his essence, an image of a child with golden eyes and hair with a thousand shades shriveling in his soul even as his senses rocketed. Her soft screams filled his head as she writhed in the conflagration of release, catching him on the shock wave, sending him into his own explosive climax.

He didn't move off her this time but lay over her, filling her, joined in ultimate intimacy, bitterness flooding him.

He was repeating his mistakes, being just sex to her.

But this had to be more than sex. She's given you total surrender, absolute intimacy… Sim, fool yourself some more.

Eight years ago, she'd given him that the same day she'd left him.

Jewel stood on the edge of her boat, watching Marúbo disappear. They were turning into a tributary, heading for another village at its furthest point upstream. The tributary would get smaller on the way so they'd taken only the smaller boats. On arrival, they'd still need to hike for half a day to reach their destination. She couldn't wait to get there.

And she couldn't wait to leave there. To leave here, leave this expedition and Brazil.

Her efforts to keep a part of her unconquered by Roque, to save something of herself to survive with, had failed. Instead, she'd traded away her one chance of survival for two weeks of absolute bliss in his arms.

She'd opened herself to him, bared everything that she was and thought and felt, let him see the extent of her love, holding nothing back but the words.

And in return, he was already withdrawing.

It had started after that time in the glade five days ago. After he'd told her what the place signified.

Had the magical place revealed to him how empty of potential their lovemaking was and had it put him off her? Did a man who didn't want children with a woman still feel repulsed if he knew the choice wasn't there?

But she'd wanted longer with him, didn't know how to give him up. And he was cutting her time, her remaining life, short.

He tried to disguise his cooling, but his endearments and light-heartedness felt strained, his spontaneity replaced by pensive watchfulness. He still made love to her, but his approach was stilted, as if he was summoning desires he no longer felt, his ferocity coming late, as if his response was building automatically, nothing to do with who his partner was.

But it was the aftermath that damaged most. Those times had been what she'd craved most with him, the sheer beauty and depth of descending together from the heights of the sensual storm, of feeling cherished and even more desired.

Now his awkward kisses and caresses, his hesitant gaze, as if he were dispensing a requisite chore, added a deeper scar each time.

But what had she expected? She'd known her attraction to him was her synthetic shell, and beauty, even when real, bound no man. Hers seemed to have lost its appeal. Now he'd experienced it thoroughly, the still visible pattern where she'd been put back together must be evident. He could now be imagining what lay underneath, seeing her with the artificial effects undone. He could be remembering her when that negligible network had been a glaring map, marring her body and face, and he'd forced himself to look, to touch, to pretend to want.

But if he was becoming sated, or even sickened, he wasn't doing anything about it. By now, she knew how compassionate he was. He probably didn't know how to end it, was trying to do it gradually so as to cause her the least pain.

And she was too pathetic to do what she should have done weeks ago. She wasn't sparing him the discomfort. And she had to find a way to release him, absolve him of any guilt or worry on her account. She had already been destroyed so it didn't matter how much more doomed she became.

He suddenly appeared on the observation deck of his boat.

Longing writhed inside her. She knew he was looking at her from behind his sunglasses, was debating whether to pretend not to notice her or whether to acknowledge her. She saved him the trouble, turned away. Then she lurched forward and crashed to her knees.

They'd collided with something!

She'd barely risen to her feet, felt the pain shooting in her knees and blood trickling down her legs, seen the ominous underwater shadow of what looked like a gigantic sunken tree, when another collision from behind sent her hurtling overboard.

She heard her name being roared out as she hit the water. The plummet through the surface was like crashing through glass. The blow stunned sensation out of her whole left side. Then a thousand razors roared along her nerves. Her eyes and mouth jolted wide on the pain and panic, and warm water flooded in, cutting off sight and breath.

She thrashed, fighting the suffocating fluid, desperate arms reaching for the surface. She reached it and it only turned into attacking darkness. The boat—it was heaving, pieces of it separating, plummeting, pummeling her under with brutal blows. She went down, and down.

Her lungs burned, her vision a backlash of murky crimson. Beyond terror, the last tatters of survival instinct drove her up to break the surface—and it was there. The boat. It was capsizing.

For endless moments, it loomed over her in a merciless taunt.

Holding her last breath, she watched it make its final descent as Roque's face filled her last thoughts.

At least this would be a way out.

For both of them...

CHAPTER FOURTEEN

THE macabre sequence slashed its slow-motion terror across Roque's vision, goring his mind.

He'd come out on deck, an unreasoning urge taking him to assure himself that Jewel was still there. She had been. Then she'd turned away. Then she'd lurched and fallen to her knees.

Alarm had hit him so hard it had delayed his realization that her boat had hit something. Then terror had begun.

Her boat had shuddered to a jarring halt then veered frighteningly. Right into his boat's path. His boat had collided with its stern with full force. This time, Jewel had become airborne, her hands clawing for non-existent purchase. A roar had shredded his throat as he'd seen her hit the water, watched it engulf her.

He'd exploded into a run, terror detonating in his gut, and had been knocked off his feet. A sunken tree had lodged in the keel of her boat and launched it at his again. His boat, still going full steam ahead on its upstream struggle, had plowed into her now horizontal boat, right in the middle, rolling it over the tree trunk, starting the unstoppable process of overturning.

His shouts had become stifled. His heart had felt like it was bursting. Horror had been killing him with every heartbeat.

Jewel had just broken the surface of the water. *Right under the breaking up, capsizing boat.*

And he was now pummeling the river headfirst, his arms and legs mad machines slicing through the water, defying the current, propelling him at manic speed, one purpose fueling him.

Shield her. Break the impact with your body. Reach her.

He didn't—*didn't.* Two seconds too late—two feet too far…

The boat crashed down on her on a wet clap of thunder that knocked him out of the water. Shock waves rippled out, conspiring with the current to swat him away—away from her—from where she'd disappeared. Jewel, gone underneath that behemoth!

"*Jewel!*"

The bellow almost expelled his life force. Then he almost burst his chest on an inhalation. If he couldn't get her out, he'd join her down there and it would be his last.

He dove after her.

He plummeted through the murky waters, desperation and terror propelling his body downwards. She could have already been swept away—the current here was swift, the visibility almost nil…

Deus, Deus… He prayed, wept. *Jewel, Jewel, let me feel you, let me connect with you, just one more time,* meu amor. *I won't ask or hope or want anything—anything—ever again. Just let me find you now—and I'll be happy to lose you later…*

Tears bled out of him, diffused in the turbid waters, somehow clearing his vision. The depths below the boat's receding shadow were littered with all the debris that had spilled out of it —down, down on the muddy riverbed… *Jewel.* Under a huge piece of hull his boat had torn from hers…

The blast of horror knocked him empty of breath. His

lungs burned. He had to go up—get enough air to fuel him all the way down, all through freeing her from her trap…

No! More minutes lost. Water filling her lungs, extinguishing her precious life. *No.*

His watery shroud was turning black… Losing consciousness… Would be no good to her dead. *Go up—now.*

He kicked his fury and dread, rocketed to the surface, struggled to take one deep breath through the quakes tearing through him, a time bomb ticking in his arteries, counting down the remaining time until Jewel was beyond salvation…

He dove down again, like a heat-seeking torpedo now he knew where to find her. He clawed his way through the impeding water, pressure building in his head with his fast descent, almost bursting his eardrums. Only Jewel, only Jewel—lying there like a discarded doll, half-buried under that twisted hulk of metal, colorless, bruised, a cut on her forehead radiating a cloud of red in the water. Blood could bring piranhas—*he had to* get her out of the water—now.

He reached her, tore the debris away, scooped her limp body in his arms and thrust frantically for the surface. He broke it, expending the last of his breath on a loud cry for help. His next breath was poured down Jewel's lungs.

He saw faces, felt hands, in the water, on board his boat, all urgent, anxious, helping. Jewel wasn't breathing, her heart beating a sluggish twenty beats per minute. He nearly died with horror every time he emptied his lungs in hers.

He stumbled to place her on the exam table, barking ragged orders.

The instruments were already falling into his shaking hands and he had no idea how but he intubated her, placed a nasogastric tube and emptied her stomach of swallowed water. Madeline and Inácio hooked her up to a pulse oximeter and cardiac monitor then started positive-pressure ventilation and resumed compressions. All the time a litany of begging and love spilled from his lips, his tears a stream splashing all over her beloved face.

Her face. It was bruised and torn again, and it didn't matter. It never had. She must live…

But, *Deus*—warm, fresh water submersion was the worst-case scenario. Inhaled fresh water destroyed lung alveoli, passed from the lungs to the bloodstream, destroying red blood cells. And if she'd been down there for longer than eight minutes, everything they were doing would mean nothing. Without oxygen for longer than that, brain cells died and permanent neurological damage resulted, even with successful resuscitation.

Suffocating with dread, he had to know. "How—how long…?"

Madeline understood, rasped, "A bit under six minutes."

"Are—are you…?"

Madeline gave a shaky nod. "I'm sure!"

They resumed their resuscitation efforts during his ragged supplications for her to fight, to come back to him.

Five lifetimes later, Jewel's pulse began to quicken. Then she started choking on the ET. He pounced to remove it, replacing the oxygen mask over her nose and mouth at once.

"*Por favor, meu amor,* open your eyes…" he prayed, begged.

And then she did. Looked him straight in the eyes. He almost fell to his knees to kiss the deck in thanks. This was a lucid gaze, disoriented, feeble, but housing her intellect and uniqueness. She was OK!

Her hand rose to the mask.

"Leave it on, *amor,*" he implored.

"Wh-wha—?" she wheezed behind the mask.

Pain clamped his body. He hunched over her, needing to contain her, protect her. "Shh, shh, *amor*, you're fine, fine."

Her hand lurched to the angry cut on her forehead and his hand jerked, catching hers before he jumped to sterilize and bandage her wound. Her fingers trembled a trail to another cut on her cheek and he again removed her hand, pressed a kiss to her lips, his rigid with the pressure of emotion. "You'll be fine, *amor*."

Dazed eyes stared at him. Then she closed them.

It had been ten days since she'd almost drowned.

Later on the day that Roque had fished her out of the river and resuscitated her, she'd developed adult respiratory distress syndrome and had almost died again.

For four days afterwards it had been like re-entering her old nightmare. So much so, she'd wondered if she'd ever exited it, if the intervening years, Roque and the full, meaningful life she'd led ever since, had not been an unbelievably complex escape mechanism of an irreversibly damaged mind and body.

Two things had convinced her this was a brand-new nightmare. Her body wasn't injured, just her face. And Roque.

For why would a diseased mind seeking escape into a dream world give her more injuries of the kind she dreaded? Far worse, why create such a man as Roque to love, only to have him not love her back and inflict such intolerable torment?

"Here comes another of my culinary miracles." Her sluggish stare panned to watch Roque pushing into their cabin, a tray high in one hand, his face alight with forced brightness. "Your last breakfast aboard before we arrive in Manaus, *amor*."

He'd cut the expedition short. And all the way to Manaus he'd been devoted to her, to nursing her back to health.

He set the tray down on her lap, brushed his lips on hers

then straightened and went to continue packing their stuff. Before he turned away she again caught that new pained expression in his eyes.

But it wasn't new. She now remembered when she'd seen it before. Right after her first accident.

She'd been so traumatized then it seemed she'd blotted it out. Now another trauma had shaken the memory loose. And now she knew why she'd blotted it out. So she'd survive.

His pity had been the one thing she hadn't been able to bear.

But had that been why he'd pursued her afterwards? Had she moved him so much he'd tried to heal her the only way he'd known how, with the best medicine there was, a gorgeous man's desire and attention? The notion *was* weird, but now she knew the motives she'd thought he'd married her for were ridiculous, it seemed like the only explanation. Why else would someone like him have looked at her then? How could he look at her now?

His behavior now only reinforced her pity theory. He'd started to pull away before the accident but was now deluging her in attention again. It seemed compassion was his strongest motivator.

Not that she'd accept it. Or endure it. If she'd been the unwitting object of his benevolence once, she'd never be again. Up till the accident she'd at least been the object of his honest lust.

But if pity had been why he'd married her, why had he been angry when she'd walked out, proving she hadn't needed or deserved pity any more, when he should have been relieved?

Easy one, that. She'd behaved cruelly. And if her suspicions were correct, ungratefully to boot. He'd had every right to be furious, to lash back.

But she knew now why she had behaved so badly. Knowing she'd never give him the babies he craved had been what had sent her mad, then vicious with pain. Believing all those lies about him had been more bearable than facing her deficiency; running away had been better than waiting for him to discard her.

And now she knew he was the one man who most needed his own flesh-and-blood family, who would be the most magnificent father, it would have gutted her if he loved her back, only to find out what he'd be deprived of to be with her. She should be glad—she *was* glad—for him, that he couldn't love her.

Knowing he didn't and hadn't loved her left out his nobility, his monumental compassion, to explain all he'd done for her. But even with the most benevolent of intentions, he must have sighed in relief the moment she'd walked out the door. He would again when she walked away this time.

As for why he hadn't divorced her, she'd also figured that out. Now that he was wealthy and celebrated, besides being the most fantastic male on earth, he must be wading in women. What better way to ward off the vultures than with a married status? He must have kept her as his scarecrow wife.

She didn't have cut and dried explanations for why he'd gotten involved with her again, none but the obvious, of course.

A long honk cut through her oppressive reverie and she found herself staring blankly at him. A gentle hand stopped her when she moved to get up.

He smoothed her bangs out of her eyes, picked up her hand, kissed it then placed a fork in it. "Eat your breakfast first *Jóia*. We don't have to jump off the boat the minute we dock."

She put the fork down. "I'm really not hungry."

She wondered at the coolness in her tones, the rock-steadiness. Must be the numbness of inescapable doom. The river boat was already docking. This was it. The end.

The pressure to make it a quick one built, made her move

the tray away, propelled her out of bed. "Sorry you went to the trouble for nothing."

Roque watched Jewel getting dressed in silence, her last words echoing in his head.

Had she been telling him something? What her every nuance had been telling him since she'd regained her health after those harrowing days when he'd almost lost her, when he'd hung onto her with all his will and life…?

Deus, he couldn't bear even the memories.

But that *had* been when her withdrawal had occurred. Up until the accident, her passion, so different from the past, so deep and giving, had *still* been at full blast. So much so he'd started to hope it wouldn't fade this time. He'd also managed to harness his eagerness, giving her the space she needed for her emotions to take root, had started to think her continued desire meant he'd been succeeding.

He'd even made peace with her episodic remoteness, accepted it as part of her character. He really couldn't expect her to be perpetually aware of him, transmitting and receiving. He'd succumbed to doubts, of course, woken up in a sweat with her in his arms, convinced she was gone, or would tell him she was going. He'd struggled to blot out those episodes.

Then had come her total withdrawal after her brush with death. But that was even more understandable. The last thing he expected now was vivaciousness and passion.

But that was logic talking. Insecurity whispered that with her frailty extinguishing her passion, the truth about her feelings had been uncovered. When her body didn't respond to his, he ceased to exist for her.

But, no! Her passion *hadn't* been just sexual. He may have believed that of her before, but not now. The woman he worshipped had such depth, such consideration, she wouldn't have given him all that intimacy, all that fire, all that *hope,* if her emotions had been uninvolved. It wouldn't have been so beautiful and overpowering without a powerful emotional ingredient on her side. And then there *had* been the companionship and laughter and dependence and appreciation.

But those were gone, insecurity lamented. And he had to listen. And burn in uncertainty. Had it been her accident? Those minutes when her breathing had stopped and her heart almost had? Had her emotions for him been in the most superficial part of her being, had they been the most fragile that they'd been the first part of her to die? And now couldn't be resurrected?

He refused to believe that. What they had, had been, *was* real. And rare. Unique. She was just depleted. He'd wait, revive her, and her emotions. But to do that, he had to have her near. But how, now the expedition was over?

He knew how, had been putting off proposing it to the last minute of the expedition. Then the last ten days had happened and it felt like a replay of the past. And now he was loath to repeat it, to offer her something she might accept only out of a need for support.

But he couldn't wait any more. He had to ask her to stay with him. He'd continue giving her space, as long as it took, take his cues from her while building up to asking her to share his life, be his wife again, and for real.

He walked behind her out of the cabin that had witnessed so much ecstasy and turmoil, headed down to the lower deck, his hands itching to grab her back, to tell her, ask her…

"Got a minute, boss?"

Berto. *Inferno.* This had to be about the charter plane he'd arranged to take them all back to Rio. In fuming impatience he watched her walk ahead, turned to Berto, spilled all responsibility into his lap and turned around to Jewel, his heart tripping—and he didn't find her!

His gaze jerked around, the irrational panic that had become ingrained in him of losing her, one way or another, turning to stupefaction.

She'd carried her bags, disembarked and was already halfway across the pier.

But she couldn't walk away—not again.

His mind froze, but his body was on autopilot, running after her. She turned at his grab, looked at him with vacant eyes. *Deus,* that was far worse than when she'd walked away before. She'd had some life in her eyes then. Being subjected to her indifference demolished him.

Say something. Put in words what she knows she means to you. "Jewel, the past weeks…"

She cut him off, her voice tranquil. "The past weeks were incredible, Roque. And they proved to me what a great thing I missed out on, walking out on you."

Elation swelled in his heart. Until she went on, "I don't have the words to thank you for everything—for saving my life, for the magnificent time together, professionally and personally. It was great to have an all-out affair and have it run its course, so that there will be no more wondering or wanting. Now that we have closure we can say goodbye with nothing but goodwill."

He stared at her, expecting her to burst out laughing and say, *Fooled you!*

But she didn't say it, continued in that rational tone, "I'm OK with remaining married indefinitely. A man like you must be beset with vultures and a paper wife is the best deterrent. It's the least I can do for you." She suddenly reached up and kissed his cheek. "Goodbye, Roque. Be happy."

Then she turned and walked away.

He remained paralyzed, staring after her as she reached one of the cabs waiting to take tourists into Manaus along its single highway. He stood there until the cab had disappeared.

And she was gone. Again. For good this time.

Jewel. Gone. For good.

And he wondered. Why hadn't his heart stopped?

So he could live with it? He couldn't. *Deus,* was that it? He'd been wrong—*so wrong*—again?

And again he'd done it to himself. He'd put himself in her path, given her every opportunity to pulverize him, then walk away.

But in the past he'd had the motivation to build himself, his vocation, and the uncertainty about her and his emotions for her, to keep him going.

He had none of that now.

This time, all was lost.

He was.

CHAPTER FIFTEEN

THE eyes that looked back at Roque were a stranger's.

He'd almost forgotten how he looked, hadn't looked at himself in the mirror, not even when he'd shaved, which he probably hadn't, for the past month since Jewel had walked away.

For the first week, duties had swamped him, running interference with his agony. Then he'd rounded up the mission's results and damages and had really started to suffer—and think.

He couldn't—wouldn't—accept what she'd told him. She'd almost died, again, and had to be traumatized. She shouldn't be on her own now. He must be with her, and if later, when she was fully healed, she still felt the same way, he'd deal with that when—*if*—it came to pass. First he had to find her.

But he couldn't. She'd disappeared.

For the past few weeks he'd torn through Rio, hired private investigators, scoured the whole country—airports, hospitals, hotels, rented residences—everything and everywhere. And nothing. Then, half an hour ago, he'd gotten his first lead.

A woman who owned a bakery downtown had reported seeing Jewel, but wouldn't give more information until she was satisfied Jewel's husband wasn't some goon.

That had forced him to stop long enough to shave. He had to try to look human again so he wouldn't scare that woman, make her think Jewel was better off not being found by him.

He slicked his shower-wet hair back, grabbed his jacket and ran to the door. He snatched it open and—and…

Right there on his doorstep—*Jewel.*

Everything about her hit him, all at once, like an avalanche, burying him, driving him to his knees in his mind. She seemed smaller, thinner, felt younger, frailer. Her hair was a blaze of luxuriant color and gloss in his dim entrance light, her eyes housing the spirit that bound his soul—and her face, the face of his every reason. It was no longer bruised, the scars less than he'd thought they would be. And she was wearing brown—*but she never wore brown.*

Deus—was he imagining her?

"Hello, Roque."

The soft, rich melody that had echoed in his memory, her voice, her presence—*her. She was really here.*

Pressure built behind his eyes, a jagged rock filled his throat, shredded his voice around her name. "Jewel…"

"I—I heard you were looking for me." Her eyes probed him, wary. Expecting he would deny it?

The upheavals, the dread, the love and loneliness and longing—it all crashed on him. He stood there, paralyzed, mute.

She nodded, exhaled a tremulous murmur, "This must be old news, then…" Her words choked as she jerked around, hurried away.

He captured her, his trembling hands sinking in her reality, fixing her face for his eyes to beseech his questions. *Are you here for me? Are you still mine?*

And her eyes gushed her response.

He had no idea when he'd carried her to bed, how they'd

become flesh to flesh. The first thing he registered was the moment he sank into her, went home, when she absorbed him into her flesh, wept for him, inside and out, and it all merged into a dream sequence. Jewel and him and union. Safety and certainty and ecstasy. Time stretched and senses bent and shattered to the gasping rhythm of abandon and the savage sanctuary of release.

Reborn, invincible with his most vital part restored and still cushioning him, anchoring his existence, he rose above her, disbelief still streaking in his system.

She was here. *Here.* His again. At least, this way. For now.

He'd take all the for nows he could. He'd put them together and make a for ever.

Her eyes were shimmering as her lips moved. He caught them, only realized when he'd drained them again that he'd swallowed something she'd said with her sweetness. He retrieved the thick words, replayed them.

She'd whispered, "I need to know. That's why I came back."

The statement sank into his mind like a depth mine. Then its import hit bottom. He wasn't the reason she'd come back?

"Know what?" he rasped.

"Why, Roque?" Her face was stained with a poignancy so sharp it cleaved into him. "Why? Why everything? Why did you marry me? Why did you pursue me during the expedition, only to keep me away? And after you had me, why did you step away again, only to come even closer after the accident? Why did you look for me after the expedition? Why did you just make love to me?"

Why ask? When she must know? She needed his total surrender in words? *Then give it to her.*

He did, pledged it. "Because I love you, always have, always will, only you—only ever you."

Her whole body jerked, then went nerveless beneath him.

He lurched up and off her, ended up kneeling, watching her crumple under the onslaught of terrible emotions he couldn't begin to guess at.

"Jewel..." he pleaded.

Her whisper stifled his plea. "If you think I want to hear this, you're wrong—wrong. I *don't*. All I want is to be with you, for a while longer..."

"*Por Deus!* What are you trying to do to me? You're back, only to tell me I'm only good enough for a longer 'affair'?"

"An affair is all *I* can give you." She shot him a weird, hectic smile. "It can be as long as you like—until you find the one you can love, would want to spend your life with..."

Would his head burst with it all? "You're the only one I can love—can spend my life with." Misery corroded him when horror filled her eyes as his confessions sank in.

She finally sobbed, "You c-can't mean that...!"

"I see you'd rather I'd told you I'd infected you with a terminal disease." It was either resort to sarcasm or weep.

"B-but th-the only reason I came back, the only reason I let us be together again, was knowing y-you don't love me..."

"You *must* want to drive me insane! Or are *you* mad? You only want to be with me if I don't love you? If I'm so beneath you that you can't bear the thought of my love..."

Her cry cut his tirade off. "How *can* you love me? No one has ever loved me, starting with my parents, even before I got messed up. Don't you see my scars? Didn't you see them back then? Is your pity so strong? Or does it somehow turn you on?"

He reeled under the brunt of her words, jerked when her hand convulsed on his arm. "Just say you're punishing me. I deserve it, for all the horrible things I once said to you."

She thought— She felt— *Deus!* All those doubts, those feelings of worthlessness, hidden, festering inside her.

Those people who'd plagued her early life had far more to answer for than he'd ever thought. The bastards had scarred her.

Yet they hadn't destroyed her. She'd surmounted her inner and outer scars and remade herself, become a magnificent human being and a force for good, the center of his existence.

But did what she'd just said mean she thought she was unworthy of his love and not the other way around? Was that why she'd believed he'd had ulterior motives in marrying her?

Of all the irony. She thought she couldn't inspire abiding emotions in him when that had always been his fear, his agony.

But after all they'd been through, after all the love he'd shown her, what more could he say that she wouldn't warp to reinforce her insecurity and drive her away?

He could think of nothing to say. Nothing, but everything.

He reached for her limp hand, prayed his confessions would heal her, let him into her trust and into her heart. He would convince her, even if it took the rest of his life.

Jewel watched words crowding on Roque's face and her world came to a grinding halt. He was about to tell her the truth.

Please, let it be anything but a reiteration of his love declaration.

"You were eighteen when I first saw you." His voice was a bass, bone-permeating caress, the most beautiful sound she'd ever heard. "It was just a few months after I arrived in the States and you were with your father at the opening of a wing in the hospital. You were the most breathtaking sight I'd ever seen."

She closed her eyes, trying and failing to hold back tears. He brushed them away, coaxed her eyes open. "I inched my way behind you and your every gesture and word appealed to everything in me. I followed you from then on, kept falling deeper for you. I longed to approach you, but I had to be realistic. You were too young. And I had so much to prove before I could dream of you. Then Michael started destroying my chances while at the same time pursuing you. The day you got engaged to him was agony. Then I discovered Michael was cheating on you, regularly, and I had to intervene. Then you had your accident. *Deus,* Jewel, I can never describe the horror I felt for you."

"So it *was* pity." The resigned conclusion escaped her. His eyes were filled only with overwhelming compassion. So now she knew.

She found she could move even with her heart ruptured. She had to leave, disappear, for ever this time. But his arms caught her in a tight embrace and she couldn't bear it.

She cried out. "Just stop. I have nothing to be pitied for, not even then. You were wrong to pity me, so just stop, please, stop."

He stemmed her indignant protest in a hard kiss, then caught her face in both hands, forced her to look at him. "It *was* a pity to see how right I was about those people supposedly close to you. It shredded me to see you so undeservedly hurt, in so many ways. What I felt was rage against those who hurt you far more than the hit-and-run driver did, *and* overpowering compassion for your pain. *And* passion. I desired you even more the more I watched your heroic efforts to get back on your feet unaided. I tried to stand by you, but you shunned me, out of misplaced loyalty to Michael. Then you set a wedding date and I couldn't wait any more. I had to claim you for myself…"

She'd been listening in stunned awe—until his last sentences, and she couldn't bear not putting him straight.

"I shunned you," she gasped, "because I couldn't bear for you to see me after the accident. I set a wedding date because

I was feeling guilty over wanting you, because I thought you immoral for disregarding my engagement and pursuing me, thought Michael deserved better, especially since he didn't abandon me like everyone else did. But I couldn't go through with it, went to tell him I couldn't marry him when I felt this way about you, and I found him in bed with another woman. He'd been using me as a bridge to my parents all along. It was a relief to find it out. I walked out and straight into your arms."

His gaze had been filling with wonder as she'd talked, but that was quickly supplanted by resignation. "I tried to offer you all the love and support that would heal you, but I can see now how wrong I was to rush you into a commitment then. I should have remained by your side, let you rebuild and heal yourself at your own pace. But I pressured you and paid for it. I felt our marriage was like quicksand. The more I showed you how much I was committed to making our relationship work, the more you slipped away. Then you got pregnant and I was so blinded by joy that I didn't see how miserable you were. Then you lost the baby, became even harder to reach, and we had that confrontation, and it was far worse than my worst fears."

Her heart had long stopped. To listen to his revelations, to try to absorb their glory—and agony. Now it punished her, pummeling her ribcage at the sight of his face closing, warding off the blow of resurrected anguish.

"It brought back the degradation of my mother's existence and my own in L.A. in the circles of the rich and bored. I had women pursuing me for nothing but lust and vicious competition, and at first I didn't understand. I didn't have much experience then, as I'd never had the time for women or anything else, studying and working myself to the bone since I was eight, providing for my mother, sparing her, since I was twelve.

Then I understood and it sickened me. But you were different. I believed in you and even more so for clinging to your commitments, no matter how misplaced. Hearing you tell me you were no better than those women, that you just used me…"

"I *didn't*." The denial sheared her. "I lied. I was just hurting so much I wanted to hurt you."

He closed his eyes, gripped the hands that flailed for him, lowered them in a vise on his knees. "And you did. *Deus,* how you did. Then, after the pain subsided to a constant ache, I'd one moment tell myself you didn't mean it, that it was a backlash at the cruelty and pain you'd suffered, that I should let you continue the growth that they'd stunted, let you heal without me, without props. The next moment I wasn't so lucid, which was most of the time, and I was plain humiliated and mad at you."

She choked on a cry and his hands convulsed around hers, then gentled, caressed their backs, his eyes intent on the action. "It wasn't all bad. It did boost my drive to prove myself and I took the years to do just that, always keeping an eye on you. Then I took over the expedition and decided to pursue you again to get you out of my system."

Yes—yes, that was a reason she could live with, that would give her more time with him, wouldn't end up with him hurt.

He raised his eyes and destroyed that hope. "But it wasn't how it worked out. You caught me again. For ever this time."

It was…too huge. Too horrible. What had she ever done to deserve his love? Tears burned their way out of her eyes. "But you couldn't have loved me. I was an empty, stupid girl, then a self-pitying, scarred mess. How could you have loved the horrible sight I made, how can you love me now?" Her hands slipped from under his, one jerking the cover to her body, the other to the healed wounds on her face, self-consciousness wringing her heart dry. "You can't. Just tell me you don't."

His eyes followed her actions, then suddenly snapped to hers, vehement opals. Then he exploded off the bed.

"You win, Jewel. It seems I have my limits and you just pushed me to them. You came for answers and you got the only ones I have. Either you believe me or not, either you take my answers or leave them. Leave *me* to finally get on with my life!" That had been bellowed.

She looked up at him, the man who meant far more than life, bore the brunt of his fury and realized. She was healed.

Any other time she would have assigned the most twisted intention to his words and run away to lick her wounds. But now she believed every word he said. Every word he'd ever said.

It should have been her life's most ecstatic moment.

She'd never known such misery existed.

But he was giving her a way out.

She'd take it, for his sake.

She rose from the bed, let the cover drop, searched his spacious, Spartan bedroom for the clothes he'd stripped off her when he'd swept her in here a lifetime ago.

She'd gathered them and was heading out of the room when he yanked her back to him, agitation setting his face ablaze.

"*Deus,* I'm sorry, Jewel. Don't leave me. I didn't mean it, I'm just—just… You need more convincing? What other motive could I have had, or have now, for wanting you, for saying I love you?"

He put her at arm's length, razed her from head to toe with a devouring glance. "What more is there? Your scars? They were just another part of you. I looked at you and saw the woman I craved, touched you and your response drove me clear out of my mind. But when you sought so many corrective surgeries I thought you wanted to go back to your old world." He ran a finger over her most prominent scar, his smile all embarrassed indulgence. "But I soon realized how stupid my suspicions were. And now I realize your physical scars were interfering with your psychological healing and you kept fixing your body until your outer image corrected the inner one."

His eyes shifted color, as if with dawning insight. "But that's not exactly it either, is it? I think your scars run so deep they're independent of how you look on the surface. So what is it? Does knowing that you were restored surgically make you feel still damaged? Do you believe that being damaged physically means being unworthy of love? Would you stop wanting me if I got scarred now, lost an arm or a leg?"

The image tore through her and she couldn't hold back, hugged him, warding off the horror. He hugged her back as fiercely. "Or did the bastards in your life convince you way before the accident that you're unworthy of love anyway?" The rumble that escaped him made her believe that any of those "bastards" would be in danger if they ever crossed Roque's path. "The parents who neglected their child, who valued her only as long as she complemented their image, who live for their whims and success, and all those who fill their circles are the worthless ones. And *you* can't be more wrong. You're everything that's worthy, everything I can and do love, more than ever now you've become all that you can be. Though I know you will continue to grow and I'll fall deeper in love with you. If you'll let me."

Her tears were a stream now. If he loved her that much then he loved her as much as she loved him. He'd be devastated when she left. It was still the lesser evil than if she stayed. She pushed out of his arms.

He groaned. "What now, Jewel? Have mercy!"

It *was* time to have mercy on both of them.

She shook, hiccupped. "I should have told you before, I *would* have if I'd even suspected you loved me—but I thought it wouldn't matter to you as I thought you never would…"

"What?" His growl was stressed, fractured. "Just tell me!"

"I may be fixed on the surface, but my internal injuries…" She gulped then blurted it out. *"I can't have babies!"*

She struggled with suffocation, but had to go on. Explain it all. "When I lost our baby they told me I'd never carry a baby to viability, that with the scarring in my uterus and ovaries there was over a ninety percent chance I'd never get pregnant again anyway. I was so devastated I couldn't bear for you to know. I begged the doctors not to tell you. Then you told me you wanted more children, had to have them, as—as is your right. And I guess I went mad…"

He stared at her for a heart-bursting eternity.

Then he laughed!

She was debating which of them had lost their mind when he hauled her to him and pressed kisses all over her face. "Ah, *minha Jóia,* my jewel, my joy. That's why you thought it was OK to make love without protection. And I've been torturing myself with nightmares of you being a promiscuous femme fatale."

"Some femme fatale, who only ever had one lover." She smothered the confession in his chest.

A shudder ran through him then he went still. A hard-breathing moment later he raised her streaming face, his eyes wide with such wonder, relief, humility—and, oh, God, so much love. "Next you'll tell me you never had other lovers because you always loved me, too, and I'll die of a happiness overdose."

His hand dug into her hair, a gentle tug bringing her eyes

up to his, his breathing ragged. "I don't care if you can't have children. I don't care at all."

"Oh, God—don't! You don't mean that. You cared before. You *told* me how much you care." She raised her voice, stopping his objection. "And even if you may mean it now, you'll care later. I saw how you looked at the baby we delivered, I understand more than ever now why it's vital for you of all men to have a family."

"*You're* my family. I looked with longing at that baby because *you* were holding her. I want to have a child only if you can have one. We can try, and if you can't we can find a surrogate mother to carry our baby."

"It would be your baby alone. It's most probable I don't have healthy enough eggs…"

"I'm *not* having a child with another woman. If you can't have one even this way, we'll adopt. Or not. I only want you. *Believe* that. I only ever wanted you!"

Sobs were now shaking her so hard she had to cling to him to remain upright. He clung back. "How do you know *I* can have children any more? Even with all the precautions, I've been exposed to tons of radiation during my experiments. What if we run tests and find out you can have children now and I can't? Would you leave me? Would you want me to leave you, thinking it was best for you?"

Her head thrashed in denial. He pressed her harder, shaking as hard now as she was. "Do you know what I thought when I looked at that baby? That if you had my baby it would prove you loved me. All I ever wanted was to know you loved me. And even now, I don't know if you do. You never told me, and now you want to leave me again…"

Sudden power surged into her, bringing her useless arms around him, protecting, absorbing his torment, confessing all. She put her lips to his chest and poured everything she felt for him, hoping it would pour right inside, fill him with peace. "Love is too small a word, an emotion—it's nothing to what I feel for you. I worship you—even when I was unfit to know my own mind. My insecurity wasn't born of my scars or my parents' indifference or people's exploitation, it was of being unable to believe my luck that you should want me, of the misery of knowing I can't give you everything you deserve."

"Just give me yourself, say you'll be my wife, for real and for ever, *minha Jóia.*" She shook her head and her tears splashed on his naked chest, mingled with his. "You're so afraid of not giving me what I deserve? Don't I deserve the right to know what I need? A lifetime with the only woman I can love? Don't I deserve some mercy?"

"Only if you promise me, if one day you change your mind, you won't stay with me out of loyalty or compassion…"

He suddenly let her go, left her staggering as he stalked over to his jeans. He put them on with precise movements then turned to her. "Fine, I promise that if one day the paternal urge gets too much, I'll dump you."

She'd just asked him for just that, but to hear him putting it in words—God!

He was going on. "Of course, since having children involves a female, and I won't have you raising my child from another woman, I'd have to marry one so she'd raise her own children with me. But since fate has already handed me my soul-mate, any other woman would be a crushing disappointment—at best. Then, when she felt how atrociously wanting I found her in comparison to you, she'd turn into a vindictive harpy who'd turn the kids I left you to have into loathsome brats who hate my guts. And I would end up leaving them and coming back to you." He raised his eyes to her. "So, as I'm bound to end up with you anyway, why don't you just save us the time and hassle?"

She stared at him, stunned.

One daunting eyebrow rose, a taunt defying her to find a response. And she did the last thing she could have expected she would do in this heart-rending situation. She burst out laughing.

He watched her helpless fit, his lips twitching, his eyes still wary. Then he folded his arms on his expansive chest and cocked his head at her. "And while we're at it, why don't you come here and coax me a bit? I've been running after you for twelve years, I demand at least twelve minutes of pursuit in return."

It was too much. Too much. Her sobering eyes told him how much, told him everything as she whispered, "Are you sure?"

"*Inferno,* you maddening, devastating, heartbreaking woman. *Just love me.*"

And she ran to him, knew she'd never stop running to him, as long as he wanted her. She was beginning to believe he'd never stop. She *did* believe he'd never stop.

He bolted out of reach, evaded her, made her run after him around the almost empty and huge room. With every parry, every burst of speed to capture him, every flash of joy on his beloved face, she felt all her worries dwindling, everything taking a fading back seat to the one thing that mattered. That she did the bidding of her man, that she simply loved him.

She had to catch him first.

He didn't let her for those twelve minutes he'd demanded. And then they were over and he stood there and let her pounce on him, let her drag him to bed, push him there and come down over his lazily sprawled magnificence.

"You're very lenient, you know?" she panted, smiling her heart out down on him, soaking up his blazing love. "I would have run after you for the rest of the night. I'd run for twelve years in atonement if you want me to."

"You'd be running in circles as I'd be running after you, too. I told you once it's a win-win situation. For both of us. And if you stick by the very simple rule I gave you, nothing can ever be less than perfect."

"Just love you, huh?" Her smile shook with the enormity of her emotions as he ran a possessive hand down her back, his eyes on fire with pride and relief. "I will. Love you through this life and any other beyond. I've loved you all these years, even when I couldn't bear acknowledging it, and it's what drove me to become who I am now. You inspired me, Roque. And I spent the years growing into someone you can love, someone worthy of you."

Roque inhaled an expansion of every pure and taxing emotion there was. He felt as if his arms spanned the earth and heavens with her filling them. He thought he'd confessed it all to her. But he still had more, would always have more, to give thanks for, to marvel at. Just knowing that she loved him. *Loved* him.

He entwined a shaking hand into her glossy hair. "It's me who had to be worthy of you, *amor.* And though I prayed you would love me, too, now that I know you do, I find it humbling. I, too, struggled long and hard with my self-worth, if for different reasons. But now that you believe I never had any ulterior motive in marrying you, now that you're trusting me with the rest of your life, this is my real validation. And, *amor…*" He tugged gently, demanding a solemn moment. "You are right to trust me. I am yours. I will live to deserve your trust and enrich your life. Never, ever doubt me. Believe every word I've said or will ever say to you."

She looked down at him for a long, long moment, as if

taking stock once and for all, assimilating acceptance into unquestioning belief.

Then she smiled, her cherished face tearful, radiant, sure. "I promise, no more doubts, no more heartache, ever again. Except if it's for you…"

"Oh, no, you don't! You almost killed me when you got it into your head you were looking after my best interests. From now on, don't think. Just love me. What do you say?"

"Oh, I can't do anything but love you. And if you were strong enough to weather my ups and downs at my worst, if you're still crazy enough to love me now, cracks and all, I'll burden you with more of me, all of me, all my life. What do *you* say?"

He gave her a practical answer, sweeping her around, drowning her in every passionate answer he could think of.

And he could think of a lot. He was brilliant after all.…

FREE!

4 Books
and a surprise gift!

We would like to take this opportunity to thank you for reading this Mills & Boon® book by offering you the chance to take FOUR more specially selected titles from the Medical™ series absolutely FREE! We're also making this offer to introduce you to the benefits of the Mills & Boon® Reader Service™—

- ★ **FREE home delivery**
- ★ **FREE gifts and competitions**
- ★ **FREE monthly Newsletter**
- ★ **Exclusive Reader Service offers**
- ★ **Books available before they're in the shops**

Accepting these FREE books and gift places you under no obligation to buy, you may cancel at any time, even after receiving your free shipment. Simply complete your details below and return the entire page to the address below. You don't even need a stamp!

YES! Please send me 4 free Medical books and a surprise gift. I understand that unless you hear from me, I will receive 6 superb new titles every month for just £2.89 each, postage and packing free. I am under no obligation to purchase any books and may cancel my subscription at any time. The free books and gift will be mine to keep in any case.

M7ZEF

Ms/Mrs/Miss/Mr ....Initials...............................
                                                                                        BLOCK CAPITALS PLEASE
Surname..
Address..
....
....Postcode ....

Send this whole page to:
UK: FREEPOST CN81, Croydon, CR9 3WZ